Forgotten

By: Esti Heller

The kids may be lost, but they still have each other

Dedicated to Mommy and Daddy. I love you and I hope to never lose you

Prologue

A cottage covered in moss and almost completely destroyed by rainfall and snow.
A path, running along beside the poor, rundown cottages.
The village was silent. Dull. Grey.
Except for the golden cries of a child.
Make that two children.
The mother held one child in her arms, smiling as she stroked her baby's head gently.
The father watched her lovingly, then looked down at the child in his own arms, smiling brightly.
Suddenly there was a knock on the door, and the parents looked at each other in alarm. The mother quickly stood up and opened a small trap door, where blankets were covering almost the entire space.
She placed the baby inside, pressing her finger to her lips before carefully closing the door.

The father walked to the door, opening it in a casual manner, but dropped it altogether when he saw the great wizard standing before him.

"Good evening." The wizard murmured, smiling calmly at the couple.

The two didn't respond.

"I'm here to speak to you two, and quickly, if I can. Please, shut the door."

The father nodded and hurriedly did so. Just after he did, the wizard revealed a hand from beneath his long sleeve.

Whispers crept up the walls, some sharp and some unclear.

"W-what was that, sir?" The mother asked nervously.

"A silencing spell." He murmured. "To keep others from hearing our conversation."

The parents looked at each other nervously, then back at him.

He smiled at them reassuringly. "Don't worry. I'm not here to hurt you. I just need to talk to you. You recently had twin children, yes?"

The mother stared at him and quickly shook her head.

He smiled at her sadly, shaking his head slightly. "I know about them, and I'm not here to take either of them away. I just want to tell you a dangerous and powerful quality about them..."

Chapter 1

Deep in the kingdom of Saffa, close by the forest, two people in cloaks walked along the dirt road. One of the two turned to the other and said, "you don't really believe he'll help us, do you?" The other kept their hidden head down and continued walking across the dirt road.

"What will happen if he disagrees?" Continued the first. The other spoke quietly, head still down. "Then we'll run away... Take refuge in the forest." The other glanced over at the forest beside them and sighed, looking back down. The two people had now reached the castle. Two guards stood by the gates, spears held in their hands. The first of the two muttered something under their breath, and the guards stepped away. They entered

the castle and made their way to the throne room, where the king sat on his throne. Once they entered they lowered their hoods, revealing a woman and a man. The woman had green, startling eyes. Her dark, frizzy hair was pulled back into a long braid, making it seem impossible for her to be a villager if a stranger had been judging her by looks. The man had red hair that hung over his blue eyes, but it didn't matter, as his eyes stood out with their startling brightness. The king raised his head with interest. Aside from messengers and dukes, he barely ever received visitors. The woman revealed a baby from beneath her cloak, a girl to be precise. The man did the same, this time with a boy. The king raised an eyebrow. There were no second children allowed in Saffa; only one child was permitted in a family. "What is this? This must be your friend's baby, right? An ugly thing it is, too." He pointed a chubby finger at the girl. The woman looked up at him, her eyes wide with a sudden fury. She started to speak, but the man beside her grabbed her arm, giving her a stern look and responded in a respectful tone. "These are our children."
The king's eyes widened with fury.

No one, not ever, disrespected his rules.
"We would like your permission for us to keep both our children, and some food for the process." Continued the woman.
The king responded sternly, "Why would I do that? You two have been nothing but trouble already! Help you raise an unneeded child indeed." He scoffed then jabbed his fat finger once more at the baby girl.
"She is the younger one?"
The man nodded.
"Then she is to be killed."
The parents looked at each other, eyes wide, then looked back at him and quickly said.
"But Arbia told us he senses greatness, in both of them! You wouldn't want to kill a source of power, would you?" The king didn't believe them. "Arbia, the greatest sorcerer in the land? Don't make me laugh." But that was pointless, since the king was already laughing deeply. "Why would Arbia waste his time on some lowly peasants?"
"Please sir, please your majesty! It wasn't our fault! We didn't know there would be two!" The woman cried out desperately.

The king shrugged. "Well, unfortunately for you, I don't care.
"We'll do anything! Please!" they pleaded. The king started to say something but was cut off by his five year old daughter, Ella. "Please father, she's only a baby."
The king stroked his beard and after a few moments replied slowly, "So you'll do... anything?" The parents looked at each other, then nodded. "Anything, just please don't kill her!" They said desperately. The king laughed, delighted. "Alright, you may keep the children." The parents looked at each other, unable to believe their ears. "In exchange for your lives." The king continued sternly.
The parents glanced at each other.
They understood. It had been too good to be true.
The woman looked back at the king. "How do we know you won't go back on your promise?"
The King shook his head and smiled. "You don't." He muttered. The woman let out a bellow of outrage and gave her husband the baby in her arms then ran towards the king, only to be held back by guards. The king glared at her then shook his head. "I have enough mouths to feed in this kingdom- I could afford to

lose some." The woman glared at him then looked over at her husband, and her glare melted into fear. The man looked up at her then sighed and looked down. "Do it, then. As long as our children live their lives happily until the day they die." The woman's eyes widened before she looked down and shut her eyes tightly.

The king nodded. "Yes, yes, of course now let's just get this over with." The woman was released and she ran up to her husband, where they shared their last kiss, careful as to not crush the baby in between them. "I love you, Max." The woman sobbed, picking up one of the babies so the man would have a free arm. The man, Max, cupped her cheek gently. "I love you too, Regina." He whispered softly. "I will see you again." Regina broke into a weak smile, as he was referencing their parting they had used when they were teenagers. The babies were taken by two guards and the parents were shoved into the chambers where death awaited them. As they were pushed the woman turned around and cried, "Be strong, my darlings, James and Dina!" The father gave a final loving look at his baby boy and was shoved into the chamber. The king watched with his daughter Ella as their screams faded away, captured by death. The king stayed looking at the small chamber where Regina and Max had been slain, then turned and snapped his fingers at a guard. "Kill the girl." Ella's eyes widened. "But father-!" The king looked at Ella sternly. "I make no promises to a pauper." He then looked back at the guard. "You heard me! Kill her!" The guard nodded and walked to the babies, holding his spear high, ready to strike. the spear came down, plunging into the baby's skin. Ella whimpered and buried her face in her hands. The king looked at the baby, anger and shock entering his eyes. There should have been blood. There should have been a cry. There was nothing. The king let out a cry of annoyance. "Why didn't it work?!" The guard shook his head, shocked, then removed the spear and tried again. This time, the spear wasn't able to pierce the baby's skin. It bounced back, dragging the guard with it. The king stood up, his eyes wide. Ella slowly removed her hands, then looked up at her father. "Father... Maybe those paupers were telling the truth!" She exclaimed excitedly. "Maybe they really are p-" "NO!" The king shouted. "Those crooks were liars! You there!" He yelled at the guard.

who scrambled to his feet. "You were faking, faking so you could save her!" The guard shook his head quickly, so fast his helmet fell off in the process. "N-no, my lord!" He stammered as he reached to pick up his helmet. The king motioned for the other guards. "Take him to the dungeons. We'll see what we can get out of him when he's being tortured." The guard's eyes widened."No... NO!" He yelled in fear as the guards dragged him away. The king sighed then looked over at the babies. "Fine, then. If I can't kill them, I'll have to make some use out of them."

Ella turned to him and asked, "You're not... Going to treat those two paupers as royalty, are you, father?" The king raised an eyebrow. "I thought you wanted to save them, my dear." Ella nodded. "Yes, but I don't want to be replaced by them," she said simply. The king smiled and put his hand on her shoulder. "Don't you fret Ella, paupers don't get a granted wish. Not from me."

-*-

The two children were brought up in the castle, neither with the knowledge of their twin that lived in the opposite wing of the castle. The girl, who's name was Nadina grew into a beautiful young lady, and the king admired her beauty, but Ella made sure she stayed as a maid, nothing more, though they did have lovely chats with the maids in the kitchen. The king paid no attention to the boy, who grew less obedient by the day, but he kept a watchful eye on Nadina when she wasn't looking. Nadina would follow every rule she was given, not once had she snuck a cherry from the kitchen; she knew perfectly well she should be grateful for the food she was already given. Although Nadina was grateful, she knew there was something missing.

Chapter 2

Nadina woke up to find herself staring up at the ceiling of the maid's area. She had slept with the other maids for as long as she could remember, and she had no intention of leaving her life at the palace. Her eyes longed to close and for her to fall asleep again, but that was against the rules. She groaned and threw the covers off herself, looking around to find the room empty. She must have woken up later than the others. She jumped out of bed the moment she realized she was late and ran to get dressed. She walked into the kitchen to find the common sight, or sound: gossip. She walked quietly into the room and sat down on a nearby chair. She never participated in the gossip, but since she had nothing better to do until their chores officially began she always listened. "So," a nearby maid named

Matilda said, "I heard that the hot guy in the west wing of the castle has been caught stealing!"
"Which one?" laughed Susan. "There are tons of hot ones according to you."
Matilda rolled her eyes. "You know which one I'm talking about." She leaned in closer to the girls and whispered, "It's the boy that comes to take the food to the king." Nadina looked up. She had always wondered about that boy. She didn't like him or anything, no. That was against the rules. But even if it weren't she still had no interest in having any sort of connection with him besides work mates. Whenever he was picking up a meal from the kitchen he'd look over at her and wink. She never responded, though, she only looked back at him until he left. He always seemed strange, yet it was still a shock that he'd actually tried to steal. The girls continued onto a different subject until a small voice interrupted them. "What did he steal?" Matilda looked up quickly. That little voice belonged to Nadina, and she barely even rose her head when they gossiped.
"Uh... Well..." stuttered Matilda.

Since Nadina never spoke, it was a huge shock to see her take a sudden interest. A shock big enough to shut Matilda's big mouth up. You'd be surprised at Matilda's shock, considering the fact she was Nadina's best friend, though.
"I heard he stole a red ruby," Bragged Kiara, as if it was incredible just to know something others didn't.
"The most prized possession of the king. He was caught running from the palace, and he was just about to make it when-" She clapped her hands together loudly. "The guards caught him. They pushed him down and hauled him into the castle. There's a rumor going around that the king put the death sentence on him." A few girls shuddered. "The death penalty just for stealing?" asked Nadina.
"It's Ella's," said Paulina. "Oh! that reminds me, Ella's gotten engaged."
Sara laughed. "That's not a surprise, Paulina. Everyone knows that. She's too beautiful to be single at the age of nineteen," she then stopped and thought for a moment. "Then again... I'd be surprised if she were single at the age of three!"

Matilda rolled her eyes. "Well, apparently you don't know that it's an arranged marriage!" That was certainly surprising. Not a prince nor man in Saffa would reject the beautiful Princess Ella. Ella had beautiful golden curls that would always shine, and people would die just to get a glimpse of her blue eyes. Eyes? You would think they were crystals.

"Well I for one am not surprised, she's a snooty one, that Ella is." Snorted Patricia, gulping down some grapes.

Nadina was a little surprised at this. No one ever dared insult the princess, but then again, it may be worth it considering she was a snoot- or at least, from what Nadina heard from the other maids. As for the stealing of food from the royal palace, Nadina thought, Patricia did it every day, and no one gave a second thought about it. Sometimes... Nadina sighed to herself. Sometimes she wished she had that kind of excitement in her life. Then she smiled to herself. Insane. She was crazy. Though Patricia wasn't surprised, some other maids were.

"An arranged marriage? Who's the groom?" asked Rebecca.

Matilda shrugged, admiring her nails. "The prince of Cora, Prince John."

~*~

Later that day Nadina walked outside to collect eggs from the chickens when she heard a few whispers. She edged around the chickens' coup, and the whispers became more clear. "They say the boy's being killed tonight, in the dungeons, the king wants to make sure he has extra suffering."

"He deserves it. No boy would be that idiotic as to steal a ruby from the princess." SNAP. Nadina looked down and realized she had stepped on a branch. The men turned to face her, but she had already run back to the coup and inside.

What was she doing? She couldn't listen to someone else's conversation. It was against the rules! She picked up an egg and gently set it inside her basket. No matter what she couldn't tell anyone this information. She looked at each chicken's nest as she walked. Maybe she should go to the dungeons, to see him one last time. She quickly shook her head. What was she thinking? She hardly even knew the boy- But maybe it would be nice to just... Get a glimpse of him?

No, she couldn't. It was against the rules. She saw an egg in a nest and bent down to get it. All sorts of thoughts were running through her head. She should go watch, but then she could be killed, along with him... She should tell the other maids, and maybe that would boost her popularity. She shook her head again. She was going crazy, wasn't she? It didn't matter anyway, she never had a chance to speak to the other maids, when would she even have time to bring it up? She turned around to find herself face to face with the boy about to die.

Chapter 3

She wanted to scream. She should have screamed, but something stopped her. She couldn't think straight, what was he doing here? He should be in the dungeons! She tried summoning enough strength to scream for the guards, and she actually had her mouth open, her voice about to come when he put his finger on her lips. "Sh, do you want me to get killed?" He paused then added, "Before I'm supposed to?" she was speechless. She never heard him talk before. It was strange... His voice was... Almost familiar. She shook her head slowly. "How-" He shook his head swiftly. "Be quiet. We can't risk being heard," he whispered. She stared at him, then raised an eyebrow and took a step back, her strength and bravery

returning. "We? There is no we. I don't even know your name!"
He smiled and held out his hand. "James."
She looked down at his hand then up at him. "What?"
He laughed. "My name. James." She raised an eyebrow then hesitantly took his hand and shook it. "Nadina." he nodded.
"Nadina what?"
she shrugged. "just Nadina."
"What about your parents' last names?"
"I don't know my parents."
"Oh..." He looked down, and for a few minutes, there was silence. "I don't know my parents either." He looked up at her and smiled. "I guess that's just something we have in common. See ya, Dina." He stopped and looked over his shoulder at her, a broad smile appearing on his lips. "Hey, I like that. Dina. Has a nice ring to it, don't you think?" and with that, he left the coup, left the stunned look on Nadina's face as she stared after him. Once she recovered from her state of confusion she ran out of the coup and looked around, trying desperately to find James. But to no avail, the boy was gone.

Chapter 4

Nadina walked back into the palace kitchen later that day to find the girls talking as they cooked. Matilda looked up and ran over to her. "Thank God! We've been waiting for these eggs for hours!" Nadina gave her the basket and walked over to the table to start cooking. The royal butcher walked in and slammed the meat onto the table. He looked around at all the stunned faces and grunted, "Don't burn it." Nadina watched him leave then turned to the meat. "So what news did we gather today, girls?" asked Vanessa. She was the type who loved gossip the most. It was never a surprise when she asked her favorite question: what new gossip is there today? Rebecca looked down and didn't respond. Vanessa looked over at her and raised an eyebrow. "Do you have something to hide, Rebecca?" Rebecca shrugged and continued to flatten the dough. Rebecca loved attention, so she was always upset whenever she had nothing to share. Vanessa should have known that, but she only cared about gossip and the knowledge of everything. Vanessa looked at her for a few minutes then up at everyone else. "anyone?" Nadina kept her eyes down as she cleaned the meat. This was her chance. She could finally get in with the girls and fit in. She just needed to say that small sentence, that James was being killed in the dungeon that night. She wanted to tell them so badly, and she was about to open her mouth when a servant from the west wing entered the room. He looked around and said, stuttering but loud, "The king has requested to see a girl named..." He looked down at a paper he was holding in his hand and squinted at the writing. "Na- Na-" Nadina looked at the paper. She recognized that name. "Nadina," she muttered, the servant looked up at her and smiled. "Yes! Do you know her?" She shrugged. "I am her," she said simply. The servant's eyes widened and beckoned for her to come. "The king needs you." Nadina looked around at all the

maid's faces, counting the amount of emotions. There was sympathy, scared, was there even jealousy? She took a moment to decide whether or not she had imagined the envy she had seen, then followed the servant out the door and into the royal throne room. The king sat on his throne, and next to him, in a glorious throne encrypted with jewels sat Ella. Nadina stood by the doorway awkwardly then noticed the king waiting for her to enter. She walked inside and looked straight at the king. She had no idea what to do when she met a royal, neither did she like the king that much. The king looked down at her and waited. A servant standing behind the king waved to get her attention and curtseyed. She stared at him. What was he doing? He kept curtseying until the king looked over his shoulder at him. The man immediately straightened and looked at his feet, his face extremely pink. The king rolled his eyes and looked back at Nadina. He smiled. "Ah, Nadina, you're here." She nodded. "Is there a problem, your majesty? Was your soup too cold?" She asked.
The king shook his head. "No, no, the soup was excellent, although the carrots were a little large."

Like your ego, Nadina thought to herself.
"There's a death sentence taking place tonight, and nothing would make me happier if you'd attend it." She raised an eyebrow. It looked like she was attending James's death whether she liked it or not.
She gulped. "Well... I have to cook your dinner with the other maids."
The king waved his hand. "You'll skip it this night."
"But... Why do you want me to come?" He shrugged. "Well, we'd like to show off a bit of your saffanian beauty, wouldn't we?" She nodded slightly. "Oh... Right. I guess I'll be there then."

Chapter 5

Nadina walked to the dungeons, the dungeons where she was about to watch something she had never seen before- a murder. Her heart was pounding in her ears, darkness creeping into her eyesight as she walked into the cold room. The king was sitting on a golden chair atop hundreds of pillows and cushions. Across the room were dukes from other kingdoms and villages. What were they doing here? She wondered. The king probably had executions around every week, why was this so special? She forced a smile as she walked over to her chair, her heart pounding more loudly with every passing moment. She sat down on the chair the king had gestured for her to sit in, which happened to be next to Ella and looked ahead, hoping no one

noticed she was shaking like a leaf. Too late. Ella looked over at her and asked softly, "You cold?"
Nadina nodded and looked down, hugging herself tightly. Ella watched her for a moment then took off her beautiful shawl, the shawl that was admired around the village. People would pay thousands of diamonds just to be able to touch that shawl. Nadina saw the glint of the tiny diamonds encrusted inside the shawl out of the corner of her eye and looked up. Ella smiled and held it out toward her, laughing lightly. "Here. Go on. We can't have you freeze to death, now can we? It's not your execution we're here to witness today." Nadina stared at her then slowly reached out toward the shawl, her fingers barely touching it when she looked up at Ella. "Are you sure?" Ella smiled softly and nodded, holding it out a little further so that it was just in Nadina's grasp if she clenched her fist. "Go on, you wouldn't want your princess's arm to fall off in the process of a good deed, would you? Take it. My arm's tired already."
Nadina smiled and shook her head, hesitantly taking the shawl. She wrapped it around herself, trying to stop the shivering so that Ella didn't think there was something wrong with her. She

managed to stop it, but it put an increasing cold inside her. She shivered and pulled the shawl closer around herself. She then glanced over at Ella and smiled, signaling she was all right in case of worry. Ella looked back ahead and sighed as she watched the guards enter the room. Nadina looked over at the king, but he wasn't there. Ella saw her confusion and smiled. "Don't worry. He's just making the royal appearance. It's mandatory during an execution. I'll be doing the same since my mother's–" She stopped and her smile faded. She took a deep breath then stood up, gathering her belongings she had brought. Nadina stood up as well. "What happened to your mother?" Well, she knew that. Queen Ariana had died of disease when Ella was just four. But she wanted Ella to be able to say it. Ella shook her head, her back now facing Nadina. Nadina raised an eyebrow. "Ella, if it hurts to say it you should try and get it over with; otherwise there's a possibility you never will." Ella dropped her small bag and bent down to pick it up, as she did a part of her face was revealed to Nadina, who realized with shock that Ella was crying.

"Ella... I'm so sorry." She bent down next to her and put a hand on Ella's shoulder. "I know how you feel. I... I never knew my mother... She abandoned me as a baby." Ella closed her eyes. She was forbidden to say anything to Nadina, so she nodded and opened her eyes, looking over at Nadina. "I'm... Sorry..." She sighed and stood up. "I need to go... It's time for the royal entrances." She started to walk then– "Ella– here." Nadina held out the shawl. Ella looked down at it and smiled. "You sure you don't need it?" Nadina nodded. "I'll be fine." Ella nodded and quickly pulled Nadina into a hug. Nadina stood in shock, unable to do anything until Ella pulled away. Nadina, still numb with shock, held out the shawl as she stared at her. Ella reached out and took it, putting it on. She then turned and walked over to a door nearby disappearing into the darkness of the shadows. Nadina sighed and walked back to her chair. She sat down and looked around. A low horn blew, and a few guards came in, standing to the side as the king entered the room. He looked around and kept walking past each of the guards slowly. It seemed as if it was a dream. The king kept walking so slowly you would've thought the world had slowed down. Nadina tried blinking a few times to see if she was just imagining it, but no. The king was still walking as slow as before. He finally reached his golden chair and sat down with a small **thump**. He sighed in relaxation and squirmed around in the seat then settled himself in a sort of comfortable position. The horn blew again and Ella walked through another door. She walked a little faster than the king but still as if in a dream. If someone would have told you she was an angel, you'd believe it. She walked in such a graceful manner it seemed that at any moment she could take flight. Her tiara lay on her head, giving off the image of a halo. Her long silk gown trailed across the floor as she walked, and her smile was nowhere to be found, but she gave off such an astonishing appearance she didn't need one. She walked over to her chair and sat down.

Chapter 6

Nadina squirmed in her seat. When was it happening? She looked over at Ella, who was sitting with her hands clasped together on her lap. The maids were wrong. She wasn't a snoot at all. There was a massive blow of the horn and about ten guards marched into the room. Another guard walked in, holding James by the back of his shirt. James looked over at Nadina, his eyes pleading. Nadina's face went red and she looked down, guilt flooding her. He wanted her to save him... But what could she do? There was nothing. Nothing she could say or do without getting executed herself. James was walked over by the guard and forced to his knees. The guard took out his sword and turned to the king. "This man has committed thieving of the king, which is punishable by death, he is now about to pay for–" "Yes, yes we all know what's going to happen now just get on with it!" Snapped the king. The guard flushed and nodded, turning back to James. Nadina clenched the armrests on her chair, her heart racing. She had half risen out of her chair when Ella turned to her and whispered sharply. "Nadina, sit down." The guard raised his sword high and swung it toward James when– "wait!" The guard turned to stare at Nadina, who had risen out of her chair. Ella plunged her face into her hands. The king's gaze on Nadina sharpened, and he said sternly, "Seize her." Ella looked up and asked, "What?" Nadina shook her head, pulling away from the guards' grasp. "N–No, please!" The king growled, "Seize her!" She yelped as the guards caught hold of her and hit her on the head, causing her to fall to the ground. Ella yelled and ran over to her, falling to her side. "Please father!" She cried. "She doesn't deserve this! If you kill her, you'll have to kill me too!" The King's gaze softened as he looked down at Ella. "I'm not going to kill her. The only killing tonight is going to be his." He glared over at James. "She just needs to be punished for what she's done."

Ella stared up at her father, fear and plead in her eyes. "Then... Then what will you do to her?" The King looked back down at her. "That's for me to know and you to ignore. She'll be fine, Ella. I promise." Ella stared up at him for a moment longer, then slowly stood up again, looking down at Nadina. "You'll be okay..." She whispered. Nadina looked up at her weakly, everything starting to fade away until there was nothing but darkness.

Chapter 7

Nadina woke up to find herself staring at the bars of a cell in the dungeon. She groaned and slowly got up, only to find herself fall back down. She crawled weakly over to the bars and tried to grasp one. Where was everyone? Where was James? Did they manage to execute him? A nearby guard noticed she was awake and walked over. "Glad you're up." She looked up at him, not knowing what to say or do. "W-Why am I here?" she whispered. The guard bent down and looked her over for a moment before speaking. "You're here because you went against the king, remember?" She shook her head. The guard sighed and nodded. "That blow must have been harder than intended. Anyway, I was waiting to bring you your lunch. I trust you won't run if I open the gate?" She stared at him and didn't answer, too confused to speak. He stood up and walked out of sight, then returned with a tray of a strange gray pile of food after a few minutes. He took out a key and unlocked the door, then stepped through. Nadina backed away and continued to stare at him. He bent down and placed the tray in front of her. She didn't take her eyes off him, in case he tried to hurt her. He looked over his shoulder to see if anyone was watching then looked back at her and placed a loaf of bread in front of her as well. "Don't eat the glop. It's sarinami." Nadina raised an eyebrow but didn't speak. He sighed. "It'll force you to tell the truth, and you're being questioned tonight." She kept her eyebrow raised and looked down at the bread. "Why?" She managed to get out. The guard smiled faintly. "Because I know you're innocent." He turned and walked out the cell, leaving Nadina with more questions than before. What did he know that proved her innocence? She picked the bread up hesitantly then took a small bite, a sudden hunger taking over her as she finished the roll. The man that occupied the cell next door said in a small voice, "you're taking this much easier than you should have..." she looked up at him.

"what are you talking about?" he raised an eyebrow then let out a quiet laugh. "Oh, you don't know?" She slowly crawled over to the bars that separated them and stared at him. "What do you mean?" She asked hoarsely.
"That boy that was just killed?" He nodded over at the ropes that had tied down James. "That was your brother."

Chapter 8

She stared at him for a few moments more then let out a small laugh. "That servant boy, my brother? You've got to be kidding me." He shook his head. "Give me proof that I should believe you." She said coldly. He sighed and looked down. "I was the guard that killed your parents." She stared at him, her eyes widening, then she looked down. "You... You couldn't have... My parents left me when I was a baby..." He shrugged. "Believe what you want, but you've been living a lie. Why would the king be humble enough to take in a poor little girl and make her his slave?"

"Because some people have enough kindness inside them to do something like that!" She snapped. "I was an orphan, and it would've taken a miracle for him to treat me like his own!" He stared at her for a moment, then laughed. "Why would a 'humble' king like that kill your parents?" She glared at him for a moment, then looked down. "If what you're saying is true... If you..." She gulped. "Why are you trapped down here?"

"Because after I had killed your parents, the king had no use for you, and wanted me to kill you as well." Nadina bit her lip to try and focus her mind on one of the many things going on in her mind. "you still didn't answer my question."

"When I took out the spear to kill you, the spear and I were only deflected by some sort of force." she shook her head slightly in disbelief. "N-No..." She glared at him. "You're lying." "Why would I?" He smirked. "I'd get nothing out of it." She stared at him for a moment, then looked down. She knew he was right, but couldn't bring herself to believe it.

-*-

That night the king, escorted by a few guards, came to Nadina's cell. She sat up, ready. The king crouched down in front of her, the only thing separating them the cell door. "Hello, Nadina." "Your majesty." She said simply. "I'm here to ask you a few questions." He said, glancing at a piece of paper a guard had handed him. "Don't fret, your majesty." She said, the slightest trace of cold in her eyes and tone. "I have nothing to hide from you." He smiled. "Good. Now," He looked down at the paper. "Where were you on the night of the murder of James Orlan?" She raised an eyebrow. Was this just a test to see if the sarinami was working? "I was in this very dungeon." She said half coldly and half simply. "Watching your guard murder him." "And what did you do then?" "I stopped the guard." She said more simply.

"Do you regret it?"

"There isn't a moment that I don't regret it, nor is there a moment when I do."

"Thank you, Nadina."

-*-

After a few days Nadina was let out of prison, mainly because she had no proof to show she was against the king, or maybe because the king was in need of her famous soup. Nadina thought to herself. She silently walked into the kitchen, where all the maids were whispering amongst themselves. The moment she walked in the whispers hushed and the girls looked down nervously. Nadina walked in, looking around. She stayed silent as she walked to the bag of potatoes and took out a knife. Matilda looked up at her, cautiously walking over to her. "Nadina... We're all so sorry." Nadina shook her head. "Wasn't your fault..." She continued to chop the potatoes, turning each to a bunch of neatly cut slithers. Matilda stood staring at Nadina's back. "If you told us where you were-" **bang.** Nadina had slammed the knife into the counter and turned to face her. "What? What could you have possibly done?! I just found out my long lost brother is dead! And you think a simple apology can help? An apology, Matilda?!" Matilda stood staring at her. "N-Nadina... I had no idea... You have a brother?" Nadina stared at her for a few moments longer then turned and closed her eyes, a few tears rolling down her cheeks. "I did..." Matilda sighed. "I'm really sorry Nadina... We all are." Nadina took a deep breath then opened her eyes and turned to face her, all of them. "You didn't do anything... It's not your fault." She turned and walked out of the room.

Nadina walked outside to the chicken's coop where she and James had first spoke face to face. She sat down by one of the chicken's nests and hugged her knees. She didn't know what she was feeling at that moment... Was it sadness? Was it shock? Was she even relieved? She closed her eyes and let the breeze coming from the outside tickle her face. It pushed back her hair and gave her a refreshed feeling of satisfaction. Of course, it wasn't real. She knew she'd never truly be happy now that she had finally found her family which was now even worse than lost... She buried her face into her knees and cried her heart out, cried away her feelings of loss, feelings of sadness, and feelings of death coming upon her. She tried drowning herself in her tears, hoping maybe if she did she'd be able to join her now forever lost family. But unfortunately, that would never happen. She didn't know how long she sat there in her tears, but it must have been a while. Footsteps approached the coup and she looked up, a delusional hope that it might be James in her heart. Alas, it was a palace guard. The same guard that killed James, she suddenly realized. She jumped up and backed away. "Don't worry, I'm not here to hurt you!" He said calmly.

both his hands in front of him to show he meant no harm. She stared at him, backing away. No words could describe the terror she felt at that moment, but also an indescribable anger and thirst for revenge. He kept walking toward her, and she kept backing away, that is until she backed into a wall. He took her arm, and she yelped and jumped away. He sighed. "Look, I'm just trying to help!" She shook my head. "You killed James..." He shrugged. "I was just following orders. I didn't want any harm with the ki–" "Well you got harm with me!" She yelled. "You're not coming any closer to me. You took my family away from me!" Her voice kept getting louder, most of it coming from her horrible anger inside. He raised an eyebrow and took a step back. "Would you come with me if I told you it was for the princess?" Her eyes widened. "Ella? What did you do?" She demanded. He shook his head. "I did nothing; but she is ill, and she has requested your presence. She's dying."

Chapter 9

Nadina ran down the hall and into Ella's bedroom where the guard had directed her. She ran to Ella's side at the foot of the bed and stared down at her, a growing sadness in her. Just when she thought things couldn't get any worse, this had to happen. Ella was as pale as a sheet, and when she looked into her eyes it was like staring into a storm. Ella lay on the bed, staring at nothing in particular. When she heard Nadina enter she looked her way and smiled weakly. "Nadina..." Nadina nodded. "I'm here... How did this happen?" Ella took a small breath and returned her gaze to the ceiling. "Th-the shawl... when I was little I-I gained a horrible illness... I would have

died if it weren't for Arbia's kindness." Nadina shook her head slowly. "Who?"
"Arbia, the greatest sorcerer in all the land." Said the guard by the door.
"Yes..." said Ella. "He gave me this shawl... But it came with a price." Nadina's eyes widened slightly, she understood. "You can't take it off... And if you do..." Ella nodded and closed her eyes tightly as she coughed. She opened them and leaned back against the pillows. "You die." She whispered weakly. Nadina shook her head. "N-no, you can't! The kingdom needs you. Prince John needs you!" Ella sighed and closed her eyes as she sank a little deeper into the pillows. "I don't love Prince John... And I doubt he loves me." Nadina looked down. "We all still need you... I need you." Ella opened her eyes and wrapped her shawl closer around her. "Will that still work?" asked Nadina anxiously. Ella shook her head. "No... But soon I will get what I've always wanted- to be free." Nadina shook her head slowly, confused, then suddenly realized. "That's why you gave me the shawl in the dungeons... You wanted to die!" Ella put a finger to her lips then slowly removed her hand. "My father

doesn't know... And I don't want him to." "But why, though?" Nadina asked. "I... I hate the idea of an arranged marriage." She whispered. Nadina sighed and looked down. "That's not something you die for, Ella..." She muttered. "I know... But my father would never understand. Please, Nadina." She looked up at her pleadingly. "Please understand. I don't even know what to do with myself anymore... Just don't tell my father." Nadina nodded. "I won't say anything." She glared over at the guard, who put his hands up in defense and said, "Don't worry. I won't say a word." She let her gaze soften and looked back at Ella, who was now coughing up blood as she shuddered. "Nadina... I need to tell you something..." Nadina nodded slightly. "Of course... What is it?" "Y-your parents... death wasn't an accident... My f-father executed them." Nadina raised an eyebrow, and then her eyes widened and she took a step back. "W-what...?" Ella's head sank deeper into the pillow as she nodded. "I-I was there... And the s-servant boy that was executed... He was your brother." She took a deep, shuddery breath then her body relaxed, and her eyes stared at nothing. Nadina gasped quietly and fell to her knees by the bed.

So the guard was right... "Don't worry Ella... We'll all remember you." She leaned forward and gently closed Ella's eyes, which would never open again.

Chapter 10

The burial for Princess Ella was in secret; the king did not want Cora to find out about the princess's death; otherwise their peace treaty would be off. Nadina returned to her maid duties, but nothing was the same. Eventually, the maids found out what happened, but they were banned from saying a word to anyone.

~*~

One day Nadina was chopping some turnips when the king walked into the kitchen. The maids looked up and immediately fell into curtsies, Nadina included. The king looked down at them all sternly then reached out and grabbed Nadina's arm, forcing her up. She stared at him. "Y-your majesty?" The king scoffed. "Don't call me that. From now on you're to call me father." Nadina's eyes widened and she looked around at all the other maids. Some had dropped whatever they were holding from shock. "You are to pretend to be the princess, we can't afford–" He suddenly looked over at the other maids and shoved Nadina out the door. "come– get out, girl! I–I mean... Ella."

Nadina walked down the hallway with the king in a daze, barely noticing where she was going so she accidentally stepped on the king's foot, causing him to swear.

Finally, he stopped and motioned toward the door. "Get in."

Nadina hesitantly obeyed and looked around. She was standing in a large room, filled with colorful decor and a bed that could probably fit about five people. There was a golden mirror, encrusted with emeralds in the corner, then two glass doors that opened up to a balcony overlooking the Saffanian mountains. On another wall, a beautiful dresser with carvings around it stood high, and on top of all that, A glittering chandelier hung from the ceiling. "Make yourself at home." The king grunted. "Because from now on, it is your home." He said before closing the door shut. Nadina could tell the king was still recovering from Ella's death, so she walked around the room and admired it's sparkles. She then looked over at the balcony. It was as if it was... Calling her. She shook her head, no. That was absurd. Balconies couldn't call people... But this one seemed to do just that. She edged closer to the balcony and opened the doors, but the sight that faced her made her nearly choke. She must have been four stories high. The ground beneath her seemed so far away, so far it seemed as if she was a giant overlooking the earth. The ground swayed, zooming in and out. Nadina ignored the calling and quickly walked back into the room, shutting the doors. She slid back against the doors and buried her face in her hands. The calling was somehow... Bringing her pain. She wanted to go to the balcony. She wanted to answer the calling that was bringing her pain, but the height terrified her. She sighed and stood up, ignoring the calling as she walked to a large bookshelf in the corner of the room. She picked up a book with no label and flipped through its pages. Blank. She put the book back and sat down on her bed, but as she did the door opened and a woman entered. "It's time for you to get ready, your highness." she said. Nadina raised an eyebrow. "Ready... R-ready for what?" The woman nodded toward the hallway behind her. "Ready to meet prince John of Cora." Nadina's heart dropped. She forgot. Ella was supposed to get married to prince John. She stood up and nodded. It was time to meet her future husband.

Chapter 11

Nadina walked down the hallway and entered the ballroom. She had been pushed and shoved into all sorts of ridiculous outfits, one including a large cape and the dress exposing above her knees, only stopping a few inches before her undergarment, smelling oddly like bananas. Now she was in a silver silk gown with long sleeves and points at her wrists. Her hair was up in a complicated knot and came down at the end. The women who were working with her had placed a glittering diamond tiara atop her head, a small ruby in the center of it. A man her age was standing in the center of the room, chatting with a plump little man. The king was sitting on his throne–he had a throne in at least every room–, listening to their conversation. The man looked up and smiled. He must be prince John. Nadina thought. He had dark hair and even darker eyes that seemed to have a sparkle from the chandelier's light. He stepped forward and held out his hand. "You must be Ella. I'm John." She started to turn to find Ella, then remembered that he was addressing her. She smiled and nodded, "I'm– Ella." She said. The name tasted strange on her tongue. Ella was dead, her mind reminded her. Ella was dead. She laughed lightly, trying to drown out her mistake. "Well… you already know that." The prince nodded, laughing faintly. "Yes…" The king cleared his throat. "Well you two seem to be starting off well but I think Ella is very exhausted from her… Hard work in the kingdom." Prince John nodded and released Nadina's hand. "Until tomorrow, then." After he had left, Nadina walked over to the king with an angry expression. "What was that?! I had him fooled!" "You were doing nothing of the sort!" The king shouted. "You were leading him straight to the secret! Next time don't be so obvious!" He glared at her for a moment longer, then sighed and leaned back against his throne. "I can't treat you like a child until you start acting like it. Will you at least try?"

Nadina stared up at him for a few minutes then nodded slightly, rolling her eyes. "Fine."

~*~

Later that day, Nadina walked back to her room and sat on her bed, removing the tiara and letting her long brown hair loose. It was a good thing no one from Cora had met Ella, actually, because she and Ella looked nothing alike. Nadina remembered Ella's relaxed posture as she handed over her shawl, the one thing keeping her alive so that she could do a good deed. Nadina shuddered and hugged herself tightly, closing her eyes for a few moments. "Your highness." Nadina didn't open her eyes. "Your highness." The voice said more sternly. That was when Nadina remembered that the voice was addressing *her*. She opened her eyes, and only then did she realize she was crying. She wiped her face as if impatiently and looked up at the guard with whatever kindness she could muster. "Yes?'" Her voice seemed flat, pressing against her grief. "I came here to speak to you."

Chapter 12

"About what?" Nadina asked as the guard closed the door behind him, her eyebrows raised. The guard turned around and walked a little closer. She then recognized him. He was the guard that had spared her from confessions toward the king. He was the one who had saved her from her troubles.
Or so she thought.
"you..." she said quietly, staring up at him. "What are you doing here?"
"I just wanted to talk," he said. "There are many things you don't know about the king, Nadina..."
"Like what?" She asked in a voice that didn't belong to her.
"Like the fact that he killed thousands of people but just happened not to kill me and treat me with more kindness than I

deserve?" She didn't like to admit it. The king had been treating her disgustingly lately but at least he had tried to act as if she was a princess. The princess, she reminded herself. She wasn't Nadina- now she was Ella. The guard sighed and shook his head. "The king isn't who he claims he is, Nadina-" "How do you know my name?" Nadina asked fearfully, almost unaware of cutting him off. He smiled faintly. "You may have the prince fooled, but he never even met Ella, so you don't have much of a job to do. as for everyone else-" He shrugged. "You're not doing such a good job." She groaned and looked down. After a few minutes, she glanced up at him. "What's your name?" She asked curiously. He smiled and bowed. "The name's Dillan." She nodded slightly, thinking for a moment. "Dillan..." She smiled faintly. "What a nice name." He nodded, looking down. "Well, my name is just a small label for me... It doesn't really reveal anything, so it's not of the utmost importance." She smiled a bit brighter. "But what if I wanted to get your attention? Should I say, 'Uh... Sir could you uh... Listen to what I have to say?'" He laughed, and they both stood in silence for a moment. "listen." He said, looking back up at her.

"I need to tell you, fast. The king has plans, plans to conquer Cora once the alliance is made. I don't know why, but he just does." Nadina's smile faded and she looked at him worriedly, her eyes wide. "What? But..." She looked down, and it all became clear. "That's... How do you know that?" She asked quietly, looking up at him. "Us captain guards have our privileges." He said simply, shrugging. "You're the captain?" She asked, interest growing in her eyes. He nodded. "Captain Dillan of the royal guard, at your service." He said, bowing again. She nodded, then looked down. "Can... Can I ask you something?" She asked quietly. He nodded and straightened. "You can ask me anything, your highness." He smiled. She smiled faintly as she glanced up at him. "Why didn't you feed me the sarnimai or... Whatever it's called?" He chuckled. "Sarinami. Created by the royal sorcerer." She nodded. "Right. That. Why'd you give me bread instead?" "Haven't I already answered this?" he asked. "well... yes, but I wanted to know a better answer than my being innocent." She said, looking into his eyes to make sure he wasn't lying, but instead of squirming like a liar would do, he smiled. "Well-" "Captain! what are you doing in there?" His smile faded and he looked over his shoulder. "I guess this is goodbye for now, princess." He said, starting to walk away. She sighed and nodded. "Until next time, then."

Chapter 13

"It's a beauty, isn't it?" John sighed happily, staring at the sunset. Nadina looked up, almost jumping from his voice. She had been watching a little lizard crawl around on a leaf, trying to jump off when she heard John's voice as if from a distance, even though he was sitting right beside her on the edge of the balcony of the second floor. She nodded. "yeah... I guess." He looked over at her, cocking his head to one side with a small smile on his lips. "You think otherwise?" She shrugged, looking over at him. "I always thought it was okay... But..." She shifted in the place where she was sitting, slowly so she wouldn't fall. "Don't you see much better sights, you know, if you're a prince?" He raised an eyebrow. "You think being a prince is all... traveling and good times?" She started to speak, then

realized she wasn't acting like Ella. Wouldn't Ella know what it was like to be royalty? Maybe Prince John was cooped up in his castle as she had been. Whatever it was, her acting was obviously going downhill, so she looked at the sun, then sighed in a tone she thought happy. "I meant to say..." she looked up at him and smiled. "It's a beautiful sight." He took a moment, then smiled a bit brighter and looked back at the sun. "One day... One day I'm going to travel to all sorts of exotic places, and discover new creatures with all kinds of originalities." he sighed happily, and a dreamy look entered his eyes. Nadina stared at him for a moment, then looked down. "That sounds amazing... I'd love to get out of the castle for once." She looked up at him and smiled. It was true. Though she wasn't really Ella, and barely knew what it was like for her, she still never left the castle, though she never found out why. John smiled and took her hand, his other was still holding him steady. "Once we're married we'll go, just me and you."
"and a bunch of guards." She muttered, and surprisingly, the prince laughed. "you're highly amusing, you know." He chuckled. She raised an eyebrow. She saw nothing funny about

what she said. It was the truth. "well..." she forced a smile. "No one's ever put it that way..." "Then let's make it a start." he said softly. She stared at him. and before she knew what was happening he leaned forward and pressed his lips against her. pushing away a strand of hair from her face. She stood in shock. then pulled away. gasping slightly with her gaze down. "Don't you think that it's a bit... oh. I don't know... Early to do that?!" she asked incredulously. He raised an eyebrow. "what do you mean?" "you just kissed me!" she said. a little louder than she had intended. Suddenly the truth of that sank in. He just kissed her. He just kissed her. who he thought was the princess. No. he just kissed her. Nadina. who he thought was the princess. "I could've done worse! Besides. we're going to get married. you might as well get used to it!" She stared at him a moment. then looked down and swung herself backward onto the balcony. "I don't know what I expected from you..." she said quietly. "but I expected better." she turned and ran inside. leaving the shocked prince with the sunset.

"Y-you didn't like how I kiss?" The confused prince called after her.

Chapter 14

Nadina walked inside the maids' kitchen and looked around. All the maids were at work, so none were in the kitchen. She walked over to her old butcher's knife and picked it up, examining it. "that won't be of much use, princess." Nadina whirled around to find Matilda looking at her with her arms crossed. She sighed with relief. "oh, it's just you."
"what do you mean, 'just me'?" Matilda asked, stepping forward. "who were you expecting?"
"oh... I don't know..." she said quietly as she looked down. "a guard, or the prince maybe..." Matilda stared at her, then laughed slightly. It wouldn't have made Nadia feel as

uncomfortable as she did then if it was friendly.. "wait... Are you... *mocking me?*"
She raised an eyebrow. "what... do you mean? I just said–"
"Yeah, I know what you said!" Matilda said sternly. "you want to rub it in my face that you're getting all the attention! That you're the big star, and whatnot! Well, guess what?" she glared at her. "celebrities never last, Nadina. Or should I say Ella?" she asked coldly.
Nadina stared at her. "what...? you're not making any sense."
"nothing." Matilda said coldly, then turned and left the room, leaving Nadina in shock and confusion.

–*–

Nadina walked in the hallway of the castle, trying to find her way to the dining room. The king had invited– well, ordered her– to eat dinner with him since she was supposed to be acting as his daughter. She looked around, then spotted Dillan and sighed with relief. She walked over to him and gently tapped his shoulder. "hey, uh–" the man turned around– it wasn't Dillan, Nadina realized. It was another guard– and grabbed her wrist. "hey! What are you–" "Sorry," the guard said as more guards came and grabbed her. "this is for– our own good." he said, then dragged her to the dungeons. "wait! What are you doing to me. I'm the princess!" the guard scoffed. "no, you're a spoiled liar who won't shut up." "I'm not a liar!" Nadina said, struggling to get free with wide eyes.

"fine. you're not a liar," the guard said as if he were bored. "but you still won't shut up."

"how do you know I'm not the princess?" she asked breathlessly as the guards tied her to a pole.

"A little birdie told us. why do you want to know?" He asked curiously. She shrugged, though the ropes binding her to the pole gave her little advantage to do so. "I think I'd like to know why you're trying to kill me, wouldn't I?"

"We're not going to kill you. We just want to punish you for lying to us." He turned to one of the guards. "give me the whip."

Nadina's eyes widened. "No... No, please don't!"

"Don't worry." The guard said, smiling sickeningly. "This is all for the greater good– our greater good." Nadina screamed, and the whip crashed down on her shoulder. Immediately the burns

the whip left appeared on her shoulder, and she grasped it as she gasped. "please..." she said weakly. "please don't do it anymore. I'm sorry I lied..." he laughed coldly and raised the whip again. "You think a simple apology will stop us now?" He grinned. "sorry, but a few words don't satisfy us." He raised it a little higher and then threw it down onto her.
Then everything went black.

Chapter 15

Nadina slowly opened her eyes, immediately spotting Dillan sitting on the edge of her bed. "Hey," he smiled, moving a little closer to her. "hey," Nadina said weakly, smiling faintly. She raised her head slightly and looked around. "what... Where am I? What happened?" "the guards got a bit overexcited with your punishment," he said softly. "I got them off you before any real serious damage was done." She nodded slightly and took a moment then looked down, then up at him.

"Dillan?"

"Yeah?"

"Why are you wearing battle armor?"

He shook his head slightly. "it doesn't matter right now."
"Dillan, please tell me." He sighed and looked down. After a few moments he looked back up and said, "Isn't it obvious?"
Nadina raised an eyebrow, then her eyes narrowed. "You're going into war."
He nodded. Nadina's nose flared, and she felt as if she were about to scream. Instead though, she took a deep breath and looked down, nodding. "King Latkis," she muttered under her breath. "And the king of Cora," Dillan added. "I have to stop this. It's my fault." She said firmly and started to get up.
"No, you need to run."
"Excuse me?" Nadina looked at him incredulously. "Run from who?"
"The King, and the kingdom of Cora. They're going to kill you."
She stared at him a few moments then shook her head slightly.
"That's ridiculous."
"No, it's not. Why do you think those men wanted to hurt you? They were ordered to, and if that's not it, then they wanted revenge on you for lying to them about their beloved princess."
"I'm not running away, and you can't make me–"

"And he'll be severely punished for it too." A guard said, stepping into the room with his sword drawn. "But thanks, for holding her until we got here."
Nadina's eyes widened and she glanced over her shoulder at Dillan, who shook his head. "Don't believe him. He's just trying to trick you." "No," Nadina said sternly, glaring at both of them. "there's just been a misunderstanding. If we work this out then-" "There's nothing to work out!" The guard said coldly. "You lied to your kingdom- to the entire Cora! Now you're coming with me." Before he could say another word though Dillan jumped forward and grabbed his ear, bringing the guard down with him. "RUN, NADINA! RUN!" Nadina stood there in shock, then mustered up all the courage and strength she had to do the one thing she did best- taking orders. She quickly stumbled off the bed and ran toward the doors that led to the balcony- the guard had been blocking the entrance to the hall. She pulled them open as the guard wrestled Dillan to the ground and ran onto the balcony, refusing to look back at Dillan, whose screams seemed to be living in her ears. She gulped at the sight of the ground beneath her, but she knew

what she had to do. She gingerly climbed over the gate preventing her from falling and kept her grip steady as she thought out a plan. She gasped as she almost lost her grip then held on even tighter, her knuckles white as a sheet. There were footsteps and she heard the string of a bow being pulled back. This is it. This is the end, she thought as tears shone on her cheeks. She then pushed her legs back off the balcony and allowed her hands to slide down on the pillars which were now supporting her life. Her legs dangled in the air as the guard released the bow. It twisted and turned as it flew in the air, then pierced the skin on the edge of Nadina's hand. Nadina screamed in pain-

and let go.

Part II

The War of Blood, Hatred, and Power

Chapter 16

Silence. That was all that surrounded Nadina as she fell from her castle room. Her eyes closed, her hope gone, her fear seeming as if it had been distinguished, because there was nothing to fear now. Her fate was as clear as it was that the caterpillar would grow to become a butterfly, but that was not what was to become of her. Death must be better than whatever it was she had then. No one would grieve her, and she could finally be with her long lost family. Matilda would not grieve her, only envy how she died a princess. It would make the king's day to hear that she was dead, and Dillan? He would move on, or just be killed by that guard. But... Would that be better? It pained Nadina to hope for something so disgusting and foul, but she wished for Dillan to be dead. She wished with all her heart that he would die so that they would be together in the next world. Her heart swelled with hope as she realized that even if that guard didn't kill Dillan, the king would. She opened her eyes. The king wanted her dead. If she died now she would give the king the one thing he truly desired– her death. Anger filled her, but not enough to cloud her determination. She grabbed the nearest branch from a nearby tree, the one that used to grow apples for the maids in the kitchen, their only meal. She yelled out in pain as the branch scraped at the gash in her hand, but reached out and continued to hold the branch as it started to break under her weight. She gasped through her pain, but no pain in the world could overcome the anger she felt toward the king, and her sudden determination to live. The trunk of the tree grew as she neared it, then shrank as the branch broke and she plummeted to the earth, still far beneath her. She screamed and flailed around, trying to grasp the nearest object that might just save her life. She caught hold of the side of a pillar that held up the castle, and wrapped her arms around it tightly. It burnt her hands and sent pains to her heart, but it was better than death. She gasped as the fall slowed, but even

as the fall slowed it did not stop the spinning of her heart and head. Once her legs reached the ground she fell to the earth. nothing in her mind clear now. She crawled toward the forest and tried to ignore the horrible ringing in her ears. But the darkness seemed to lick her up. lick by lick.
until there was no more than the darkness.

Chapter 17

Why is the grass green? Why does it matter that grass is green, and not that the butterfly is blue? Or red? Or blue with red, with bright little spots of yellow flickering against the warm sunlight.

Maybe the world will never know. Maybe some mysteries were meant to be kept... Mysteries. Most times the world will only wonder about one thing, when really it must be focused on the other. Times like these were such a moment. Nadina had woken up to find herself in the forest; the one villagers feared to look at. It was known to be either a refuge, or a land that devours its inhabitants. She was now weakly wandering the forest.

hesitant to touch anything. One move- just one- could send her plunging to her doom, or it could alert one of the many creatures living here- or worse. She was wondering about how the air was so clear here, when really she should have been wondering how she was still alive. Because it was a fine story, indeed... She walked in a shallow stream, and didn't care for the cold feeling that entered her shoes. She was free. Free of the restraints the castle had always kept on her. Free to sing when she wanted, free to feel however she wanted, free to eat what she wanted.
The only thing was that her choices... Even the smallest option- could destroy her freedom forever.
-*-

Nadina pulled yet another mango from the large tree and went to the fallen log by the stream where her stash awaited. She had been living in the forest for three days now, and she knew that it was true, what they said about the forest being the perfect refuge, and false that it should be feared. She hadn't seen any sort of creature that was to be feared, nor a living soul besides an ordinary squirrel or bird. Her wounds had healed over the two months she had been living in the forest. She sat down on a fallen tree and sank her teeth into one of the mangos. She had grown a great liking to the feeling of the mango's juice spilling down her cheeks, so she always let the juice sit on her chin for a while before she brushed her hand across to dry it, then flicked the remaining juice off her hand. The juice flew from her hand and fell to the ground by a few pebbles. She watched it, and then her heart quickened as the pebbles started to shake. She turned around and gasped. The creature standing before her had large horns, sharp claws and dark, thick fur. It had great yellow eyes that seemed to make the whole forest glow against the dark of night. "s-steady... Big... Monster... Thing...?" she said slowly, her voice shaking under all the fear pushing against it. She continued to back away, then slowly, inching towards it, picked up a rock and threw it at the beast. The beast stopped a moment as the pebble landed on his nose, then shook his dirty mane then prepared to pounce. Nadina, frozen in shock could do nothing but watch as the foul creature, so close she could feel it's revolting breath on her face, opened it's ferociously large mouth, revealing it's terrifying teeth. Suddenly, out of nowhere a rock flew into the the monster's mouth and down its throat. The beast paused, then loud choking noises escaped its throat. A girl stepped out of the shadows with the slingshot that had released the rock and took out a small dagger from her belt. She ran over to the beast, letting out a human like roar and plunged the blade into the monster's skin. The beast let out a ferocious roar and fell to its death upon the earth. Nadina sighed with relief and looked up at the girl. "Thank you..." she whispered gratefully. It was then that she noticed the girl's features. The girl had long, slightly frizzy light brown hair in a braid, green eyes and dark freckled skin. She wore tattered clothing, a long sleeved brown shirt and old brown pants, ripped at the knees. She also wore a belt filled with weapons on it, like a dagger, slingshot, sharp ended boomerang and weapons Nadina didn't know or had an interest in the name for which. "What the heck were you thinking, being out here alone?!" The girl asked sternly.

"Er- I was er..." Nadina thought for a moment, then looked back at her. "I ran away from the castle."

"What were you doing at the castle?"

"I er..." Nadina looked at the ground. What should she say? If she told this girl the exact reason she had run away, she might turn her in, but if not she could finally have some way to actually live in the forest! "I was posing as the princess... When the kingdom of Cora discovered this they planned to kill me, as did the king of Saffa, so I ran away..." She took a moment, then looked up at the girl, expecting her to grab her and take her back to the castle, but she just rolled her eyes and grabbed Nadina's arm, glaring up at her.

"Lying won't get you anywhere, 'princess.'"

Nadina took in a sharp breath, her heart pounding. The girl took a moment, then released her and stood back. "You're not... You're not going to take me back?" Nadina asked weakly, her heart still pounding in her ears.

"Back to what?" She rolled her eyes. "You're crazy fantasy world? No, I'm doing you a favor. Sending you to where you belong." She pulled out a dagger from her belt and flipped it so that it pointed it toward her, growling. "No one comes into these woods without a reason and gets out alive." She stood still for a moment, then yelled and ran toward her with the knife, but

Nadina rolled out of the way and the dagger hit a tree. The girl stared at her knife, which was now hidden by the tree, then let out a growl and pulled out.
"Nice reflexes. But how long can you last?"
She threw the knife in Nadina's direction, only to see a rock throw it off its path.
"Watch it, Lee." Said a quiet voice from the shadows. A boy that looked like he was seventeen or more stepped out of the shadows. He had brown hair and an eyepatch over his right green eye. "I'm Reuben. The whiner over there is my partner, Lee."
Nadina stood still, panting as she stared at the newcomer.
"Can't you see I'm trying to get my kill of the day?!" Lee growled, throwing a dirty look in Reuben's direction.
"Looks like you've already gotten it." Reuben nudged the dead beast with the toe of his boot. "As well as the many others you've killed this morning."
"Well, there's not much else to do here!" She said in defense, seeming to forget Nadina for a moment. "Nothing exciting goes on around here!"

"Listen to me, Lee. This girl will not be the key to your happiness if you kill her!" Reuben sighed and rested his hand on his forehead. Nadina watched them both for a moment, then carefully started to back around the fallen tree behind her so she could make a run for it, but immediately stopped when Lee's dagger hit the wood just inches away from her right ear.
"Don't. Move." Lee said sternly, glaring over her shoulder at her.
"Lee." Reuben started towards her.
"What?!" She asked sternly, turning her gaze to him. He stayed silent for a moment, then looked down.
"Maybe we can bring her back to you-know-who." You-know-who? Nadina wondered. Who was that? Who were they talking about? Her heart was thumping in her chest so loudly she was afraid the girl called Lee would throw another weapon at her, and actually hit her. Lee thought this over for a moment then threw her head back and laughed.
"Yeah, like he'd want a palace wannabe like her!" She jabbed a finger at Nadina, whose blood turned cold.
"We don't know! She could be the missing... You know..."

"And she could be a spy!"
Reuben looked Nadina's way, who shrank under his gaze, then looked back at Lee.
"I don't think so." He muttered.
Lee watched him, her gaze ice cold, then sighed and nodded slightly. "Fine. But if she's no use to him, then I get to kill her, right?"
These people are mad, thought Nadina.
"Lee..." Reuben said warningly, giving her a look.
"Alright, fine." She sighed and gave in, walking away. "But don't expect me to be happy about this." Reuben watched her for a moment then looked over at Nadina. "No one asked you to be." He muttered under his breath, then walked over to Nadina. "Come on." He extended his arm for her to take. She looked up at him for a moment, hesitant. Should she go with him? She looked into his bright green eyes, then her eyes moved to his messy hair, and couldn't help but feel some sort of remembrance... Something that made her want to trust him. She took one last moment before raising her hand and dropping it gently into Reuben's hand. He raised an eyebrow, then smiled

faintly and led her down the forest. Nadina looking around in fear as he did.

Chapter 18

"Face it, Reuben. You got the wrong tree!" Lee insisted as she watched Reuben walk around a wide tree for the third time, in search for something. The tree was large, wide at the sides and covered in moss. "No, I know it's here somewhere... Aha!" Reuben felt a small knot on one of the sides of the tree and pushed onto it. To Nadina's great surprise the knot sank into the tree and stayed there. The ground then began to shake, and an opening formed in the ground. There were no stairs, just a big, circular hole, and the ending was covered in darkness. "W-we're jumping through that?" Nadina asked in disbelief, staring down at it. Reuben nodded, glancing over at her.

"Is something wrong with that?" She raised an eyebrow as she looked up at him, then shook her head slightly.
"No... I guess not..."
He nodded then took a step back. "After you."
She looked up at him and smiled faintly, hugging herself tightly before looking down at the hole, hesitating before jumping through. She fell for a few seconds, then landed on the ground of the room she found herself in. She looked around then slowly stood up, looking around fearfully. Reuben landed beside her, a little more in control than she had been, and stood up. "Come on." Lee walked over to them, her arms crossed. "I'd like to get this over with." Nadina watched her for a moment, then followed as Lee and Reuben started walking away. The room was dark and eerie, yet filled with people, all with tattered clothing and messy hair, dirt on their bodies. Nadina watched as a woman fed a rotten banana to a small girl who gobbled it down in just five seconds, then she quickly turned her gaze to Lee and Reuben who were walking in front of her, deep in a low conversation.

Finally, Lee turned to Nadina. "Stay here." She said quietly, then turned and disappeared into the shadows. Nadina looked around at all the people in fear, her heart pounding in her ears.
"Don't worry." Reuben rested his hand on her shoulder gently, sending chills down her spine even as he was smiling down at her. She looked up at him, trying her best to smile. She didn't know whether or not she could trust Reuben, but at the moment this was her only real chance at survival- and besides, she was getting tired of having mangos all the time.

-*-

After a while, Lee returned and told Nadina to get up. "Come on... He wants to see you." She kept her voice low, and Nadina couldn't help but feel nervous. He? Who was 'he'? She bit her lip and nodded, quickly standing up to follow her. Lee led her down a dark passageway, until they reached yet another dark room.
"She's here." Lee nodded toward Nadina. Nadina squinted, then realized that Lee was speaking to a boy in the room, whose

back faced them. The boy looked over his shoulder at them, saw Nadina, then turned back away.
"Leave us." The boy muttered, keeping his back toward them. There was something familiar about that voice... But what? As soon as Lee left the room the boy turned to face Nadina, and she realized that he was her age.
The boy had brown, messed up hair and blue eyes that seemed to have once had sparkle, but was now lost. The boy did not speak, yet there was something familiar about his mere presence... Nadina took a closer look at the boy, then a sour, yet soft taste landed on her lips.

"James..." She whispered, the words leaving her mouth without her knowledge of it. The boy stiffened slightly at the name, but nodded.
"Yes, James."
Nadina hesitated, then slowly took a step forward.
"D-do you know who I am?" She asked shakily.
He took a moment, then nodded. "Nadina."

She took a deep breath, then took another step forward and wrapped her arms around him. She stood there, hugging the last of her family tightly, then felt her brother's arms close around her. No words passed between them, but Nadina knew—this was her brother, holding her like she'd always hoped for her family to do.

Chapter 19

The two twins stood together for what seemed like forever, then finally James pulled away.
"What are you doing here?" Nadina asked, her eyes wide. "You were–"
"Dead?" James nodded. "I know. Stealing the jewel... Wasn't exactly my idea." he smiled mischievously, the same smile Nadina was so used to.
"What do you mean?" She asked in confusion.
"Well... It was kind of... Ella's idea."
"What?!" Nadina exclaimed, staring at him.

"No, no, it wasn't anything bad! She had a plan! To get us out of the castle!"
"Where was I gonna come in there?" She asked, her anger at Ella growing.
"Well... How did you get out?"
"It doesn't matter how I got out. Ella was dead when it happened! It couldn't have been–" Suddenly she stopped. Was it a plan that whole time? Was that the reason Ella had given her the shawl? Suddenly it made sense.
Ella had died so that she'd have to pose as her, and when everyone found out the guards would come try to hurt her...
And she'd escape...
But then was meeting Dillan a lie, too?
"Ella's... dead?" James asked in disbelief, staring at her.
She looked up at him, taking a moment before nodding.
He sighed and looked down, closing his eyes.
"You didn't tell me how you escaped dying."
"Ella gave me pixie dust."

Nadina looked up at her older brother, nodding and looking down. She felt as if she should say something, something a twin would say to their own. But nothing came to mind.
She sighed quietly. She knew nothing about family. She closed her eyes for a moment, then opened them and pulled away.
She didn't know anything about family, that was true, but it didn't mean she couldn't learn.
"James, about ou- I mean, your parents-"
James shook his head and smiled faintly. "I know, sis."
Nadina stopped short and looked up at him, her eyes wide. "H-how...?"
"The morning I stole a jewel from Ella she called me to her room, she told me everything. She told me that you and I deserved a second chance, but she forbid me to tell you anything." He smiled and spread out his hands, then let them fall to his sides. "That's why I created this whole rebellion. Isn't it great?" He stepped forward and took her hands in his. "We can avenge our parents' death!" Nadina looked down, thinking hard. She remembered how hard it was for her to accept the fact that King Latkis had killed her parents, but

killing him and the castle guards... Then again, she realized that there had been a flame inside her, begging for food so it could expand inside her, eating at her heart until she would give in, and now it had begun to nibble, which would soon turn to devouring.

She took a moment, then looked up at James and smiled. "It is." The moment she said those words was the moment something appeared at the front of her mind. There was an innocent behind the castle walls... But who?

"Er... I'm gonna go see if I can find Lee and Reuben." With that said, she turned and walked down the hall, pondering over her thoughts. Nadina remembered that this someone was important to her... Very important. She shook her head and pushed it to the back of her mind. She continued walking, and as she passed certain people, a little girl grabbed her arm, holding her back. "Are you the girl who pretended to be the princess?" She asked, her eyes wide. Nadina stood still for a moment, unsure of what to do. How did she even know about that? Wasn't this place secluded from the kingdom? One part of her, a wild, terrifyingly dangerous part of her she never wanted to unleash wanted to tell her to leave her alone and wrench her arm away- she had no experience with little kids- but another part of her, a quiet, shy part just wanted to ignore her and walk away. She was shocked at both of these instincts. She never wanted to do either of them. Instead, she nodded and sat down beside her.

"I'm Nadina. What's your name?"

She was surprised to hear how easy the words came out, and how sophisticated and confident they sounded compared to her quiet, unsure voice that had belonged to Nadina the maid.

"I'm Janelle."

"That's a beautiful name, Janelle." Nadina smiled down at her, unsure whether to take her hand or not, but in the end she decided against it.

But the unjoined hands didn't matter, not when Nadina saw Janelle. The little girl was positively glowing, and her eyes gave off such a sparkle Nadina felt like she was looking straight into the great big universe, which now seemed so much more beautiful once she was looking more closely.

It was like G-d had taken a bunch of stars and placed it right into those beautiful brown eyes. After a moment, though, her smile faded and she looked away, and Nadina wished so hard she could bring it back somehow.
"Do you think someday I could be like you?" She asked hopefully, looking back up at her. Nadina was quiet for a moment, then took her hand and looked up at her, knowing this was the right time. "W-what do you mean?"
"You got to be a princess. Lee told me."
Nadina looked around the cave room, finding Lee sharpening her weapons on the other side.
"Well, that was-"
"But every time I try to be like you, it backfires, and I end up like a clutz."
Nadina was stumped at this- she had no idea anyone had ever looked up to her... Then again, she had no idea anyone really knew about her.
"That's the thing, Janelle. I'm not anything special..." She looked down. How could Janelle even want to be slightly like her? She had no identity. "Most of the time I was in the castle

I was a maid, living a humdrum life until the princess died and I had to take her place... You don't want to be like me. You need to be yourself."
"But..." She sighed and looked down. "I don't- don't tell my mom this, but- I don't think I know who I am after all this pretending..." She whispered, and Nadina could see there were tears in the girl's eyes.
"Pretending?"
"We're all hiding from the king's army. We're not even considered villagers anymore, because we betrayed the king."
She leaned forward and gently wiped Janelle's tears away, then smiled softly. "Then let's find out who you are." Janelle sniffed, then wrapped her arms around Nadina tightly, and the two sat in a tight embrace. "You'd be a great queen, Nadina..."
Nadina let out a soft, small laugh as she kept her arms around her, then pulled away, keeping her hands on the little girl's shoulders. "So would you, Janelle." Janelle glowed when she heard her name, then stood up. "Go to your mom now," Nadina said softly, and watched sadly as Janelle ran to her mom, giving her a big hug.

"Makes you think about what mom was like, huh." Nadina spun around to see James then sighed with relief and nodded, looking back at Janelle and her mother. "Yeah..." James put a hand on her shoulder, then looked around at all the people there. "Most people here aren't even here to help..." He said sadly. "Just for protection, which of course we happily provide." He added quickly, looking down at her. "It just makes things harder..."
He sighed and ran a hand through his already messy hair, looking frustrated. Nadina watched him sadly, wishing she could help him.
James stood silent for a moment, then turned to Nadina and smiled, but Nadina could see how feeble his attempt turned out.
"James, I'm..."
James was staring back at the mother and Janelle now, but when he heard his name he snapped to.
"But now that we have you we can start the invasion."
He spoke cheerily, or at least, Nadina thought, a little more cheerily than he had just been a few moments ago.
"Invasion...?" She asked quietly, confused.

"We're going to take the kingdom." He said simply. "and make sure everyone gets the food and shelter they need." Nadina was touched; she had almost stopped believing there had been anyone like that anymore. but even so. she still had her doubts. "James... That's amazing. but... It's not as simple as you think it would be." She whispered, lowering her gaze. He looked up at her and shook his head. "I don't care how hard it will be. Don't you want to help these people. especially after seeing them in person?" He asked quietly. raising an eyebrow. She couldn't believe he would doubt her like that. Of course she wanted to help! But all she could manage to do was nod. He seemed satisfied for a moment. so she decided to leap in. "James. why were you wait-" James quickly put up his hand for silence. Nadina looked around as everyone in the cave-like home went silent. Above. muffled voices could be heard. footsteps making the ground ceiling shake slightly. "Guards..." James muttered before moving around the room. telling everyone to be silent. In just a few seconds he returned to her side.

"Stay here." He said sternly, and Nadina was instantly terrified.
Was it really that bad?
James took a moment, making sure she'd stay put then embraced her. She felt his arms around her, and, as he did, realized how dangerous it was for these people to resist... How dangerous it was for them even to live here, outside the monarchy's watchful eye, and she realized she was now one of these people... Only her situation was at least two times worse.
Then she looked around at all the people there, and realized she was being selfish. Most of these people were either injured or harmed, and while they were barely surviving they were being hunted down. James pulled away and gave her what was supposed to be a reassuring squeeze before turning and climbing up the hole leading to the outside, Lee, Reuben, and barely a handful of others climbing up behind him. Nadina stood quietly for a moment, then heard shouts from above and ran below the hole, starting to climb up when someone grabbed her leg. Nadina was about to shake the person off her leg when she saw it was Janelle.

"Please don't go up there," Janelle said as her mother came, trying to pull her back gently. "It's not safe." Nadina looked down at her for a moment, then up above as she heard the clash of swords. "I have to." She said quietly, taking a last glance at Janelle's mesmerizing face before climbing the hole and onto the battlefield, gasping. The guards looked the same; with blue and gold uniforms, silver swords, and black hiking boots. But this time, they were accompanied by Coranian guards. Nadina recognized their black and green uniforms. A man with dark skin and bright blue eyes was battling James, swinging his sword at him while James ducked and swung his leg beneath the guard, causing him to topple over. She watched as James slowly rose, panting, as another guard spotted her and came running at her, his sword raised. She looked up at him then quickly hopped out of the entrance to the cave and ducked in between his legs. The soldier stumbled, then looked over his shoulder at her, his eyes wide with anger and slight confusion. He must not be used to letting people get by him so quickly, she thought as she dodged his next attack, barely coming in contact with the sword by the loose strands of her hair. She gasped out in surprise. How was she not dead yet? It was like a sudden new profound energy had filled up her entire body, coursing through her like a strange hot substance crawling down her throat and into her lower body. She glanced over at James– something seemed to be going on with him too, unless that was his usual fighting style. But no– no one could possibly dodge a sword plunging like that. He seemed to be surprised he could have done that too, and glanced her way. They exchanged a short nod– just one nod that said so much. Keep going, no matter what surprises are in store.

She could tell there was some lingering anger inside him that she disobeyed him, but hadn't her disobedience helped him? She shook her head and snapped back into the present just as another guard came running at her, but she grabbed his arm and used his unbalance to pull him toward her and slipped away so he crashed into one of his fellow guards. She was amazed. If only she had this strength and power at the castle, she could have taken down that guard– she could have helped Dillan... She could have saved him from whatever cruel fate he was sent to. She could have stayed back, could have stayed at her more than luxurious home, safe and warm and untroubled by the rebellion, oblivious to the fact that she had a twin brother... That he was the reason for this resistance, going against all they used to stand for. She shook her head and gasped when she saw that that was the last of the guards– all of them were on the ground, none dead, all but one unconscious. The one conscious one was mumbling things, his eyes darting around at all of the rebels– including Nadina– wildly, and drooling. Nadina looked over just in time to see Lee flexing her wrist muscles, glaring down at the guard with a mean look of satisfaction written all over her face, making her look dark and dangerous in the shadows of the trees, but it wouldn't be the first time Lee had managed to scare her. She took a moment, then looked over at Reuben, who was panting slightly and looking down at the guards, analyzing their faces. There were a few other girls her age there, the others men. But she had seen other women down in the cave, perhaps too weak to participate in the fight. James walked over to her, grabbing her arm and pulling her to face him. "What were you thinking, coming up here?"

"I wanted to help. You sounded hurt!" She protested, trying to wrench her arm out of his, but his grip was too tight. "You should have listened to me." He said quietly, releasing her then turned and jumped down the entrance. Nadina watched, her eyes showing her hurt then looked desperately at Lee, who simply shook her head and walked past her, followed by Reuben.

Chapter 20

That night Nadina lay on the cold ground, tossing and turning in her small spot. She sighed shakily and made to sit up when she noticed someone nearby stirring- and when she squinted she saw it was Lee. Then a second figure came into view.

Reuben.

Nadina was confused. What were those two doing in the middle of the night together?

"Hey, how're you holding up?" Reuben asked quietly, walking over to her.

Lee shrugged. "As good as ever. How about you?" She whispered.

He nodded. "fine."
She smiled and wrapped her arms around his neck, pulling him close to her and pressing her lips against his. Nadina watched, her mouth dropping open in shock from where she lay on the ground. "I love you... But can I be honest?" He whispered, pulling away from her and looking down at her.
Lee nodded. He took a moment, then sighed and looked down, closing his eyes. Nadina had never seen Lee so... Vulnerable. So loving towards anyone. But then again she had only known Lee for a day.
"I want to leave this place... And I know this is all for the good of the people, that we're saving the lives of many, but I don't want to risk losing you... My everything. Missing the chance to start a family..."
Lee looked up at him. "Y-you want to start a family?" She whispered, her eyes filling with tears. Reuben smiled faintly and nodded. Nadina watched as Lee looked down and closed her eyes, breaking into a wide smile and nodded quickly.
"Yes..." She whispered.
Gross, Nadina thought.

Reuben smiled and moved in for a kiss, but Lee put her fingers up and stopped him. "But not now. Not here. We're going to war soon, Reuben... We can't do this just yet." Reuben took a moment then nodded. "Uh... Right. Yeah." He looked to the side, then cleared his throat. "Well, whenever you're ready... I'll be here." She nodded, keeping her gaze down. Nadina watched then quickly closed her eyes, trying hard to fall back asleep.

Chapter 21

Nadina slowly stirred awake and looked around wearily. Her vision slowly cleared, and she propped herself up one elbow to give her a better view. Lee was sitting in one corner sharpening her dagger, while Reuben sat calming a little girl who was shaking so uncontrollably her features were blurred to Nadina. They were such opposites that for a moment Nadina believed that what she saw last night was a dream, but she glanced over at the dirt floor and saw faint footsteps engraved in the soft earth, so however great of a coincidence that could have been, Nadina knew what she saw had actually happened. She looked around for James, but her brother was nowhere in sight. She sighed and reluctantly stood up, stretching her arms against the strain of her tense muscles. She yawned and looked over at Lee. Well, if she was going to stay here, she might as well make sure she had no enemies. She bit her lip, and made her way over to Lee, who either took no notice of her, or was pretending she took no notice. Nadina sat down and watched sparks emit from the dagger as it lost contact with the solid rock Lee was using to sharpen it, then cleared her throat.

Silence.

She raised an eyebrow, then cleared her throat again.

"Yes, your highness?" Lee said icily, glaring up at her.

"I'm not a highness," Nadina said quietly, slightly taken aback at the smooth ice so obviously coming from the girl's mouth. Why, if anything, she'd have expected flames. "Or any royal, at that... I was just hoping we could... Talk?"

Lee raised an eyebrow then took a moment before nodding.

"Sure... I guess." She muttered. Nadina smiled in relief, knowing this was her one chance to get on Lee's good side. She expected to get right on talking, but Lee stayed silent, continuing to sharpen her dagger, which was starting to get on Nadina's last nerve.

"Uh... What made you join the rebellion?" She asked awkwardly, running a finger along her knee. Lee shrugged.

"Protection..."

Nadina raised an eyebrow, waiting for an explanation, but it didn't come.

"Against... What?" She asked quietly.

Lee took a moment, then looked away from her.

"None of your concern." She seemed to want to say, but instead, and as Nadina could tell, her surprise, her words came tumbling out of her mouth, as if she had been holding in her feelings for a very, VERY long time. "... When I was a little girl, about five, my father died of illness. I thought I'd lost everything, but that was just the beginning." She went silent for a few moments, then closed her eyes tightly, and Nadina saw in shock a tear fall onto her lap. She had thought Lee invincible, which seemed silly, especially now that she was sitting next to a crying Lee.

"My mother was pregnant."

She couldn't help it–she gasped, then quickly covered her mouth as if hoping that would cover up for her obvious mistake. Lee didn't seem to notice, though.

"But... How?" Nadina asked quietly, then stopped.

"She fell in love," Lee muttered like this was obvious, keeping her gaze away from her. "It was hard. We were all desperate for food, for a place to stay... And the guy she loved stole pretty much all we had and left." Nadina stared at her then looked down. How could she have been so stupid? Had she honestly thought that Lee had lived a normal, food-filled life like she had?

"I–I'm sorry..." She whispered sincerely, looking down. What else could she say?

Lee shook her head. "I met Reuben while hunting with my brother." Nadina instinctively looked around the room to see if there was anyone resembling Lee, but to no avail. She raised an eyebrow, then looked back at her. Lee shook her head, noticing this motion.

"There's no point looking for him... He died a few years ago. We were hunting for some food and a marder found us, and..."

She blinked back tears, which seemed to be stinging her face. Nadina, still shocked by this new look at Lee, sat there with no idea what to do, so she awkwardly reached out and patted her on the shoulder, yet even in doing so Lee still didn't seem to notice or care. Suddenly she sprang up. "He was so stupid!" She exclaimed, her face shining. "Always looking for adventure and danger, when he was already enough trouble for my mother! He was the reason she was executed! And what does he expect? A giant king sized adventure waiting around the corner for him to gulp down without a moment's hesitation!" She gulped, then sat down, and yet, in spite of her tragic meltdown, she was still sharpening her blade, though at top speed. "Lee-" She started, but Lee cut her off with a loud sob, and then, out of nowhere, turned to her and hugged her so tightly Nadina thought she might suffocate- from shock and lack of oxygen. "L-Lee-" She choked out, sure that her face was turning blue. "Please-" Suddenly Lee whispered something in her ear, and despite her inability to breathe at that moment, Nadina could hear every word Lee uttered at that moment loud and clear.

"I'll teach you, just– don't tell anyone about this."

Chapter 22

"You're holding the bow all wrong, Nadina, keep it straight! No, now the arrow's all crooked!" Lee groaned as Nadina struggled to cooperate with the dangerous yet delicate routine the bow and arrow required from her.

"If you think it's so easy, why don't you try?" She asked fiercely. They had been meeting up at night for weeks, and both were beginning to tire and grow angry with the constant lack of sleep and truth.

"Fine, I will!" Lee snatched the bow and held it up, pulling the bowstring back and then releasing it so that the arrow shot forward, slicing the chilly air like a knife and landing in a perfect bullseye on the target. Nadina, dumbstruck, watched, then snatched the bow back and went to fetch another arrow, grumbling, "That was just luck."

"You okay, sis? You look a little tired." James said softly, watching her with a worried expression in his eyes. She looked up at him and nodded, smiling faintly. "I'm all right." She said quietly.

Over the next few weeks, Nadina's fatigue only grew, unlike her archery success.

Nadina sat down on the log, groaning. "This is pointless!" She moaned. Lee walked over.

"It's not pointless if it teaches you to survive." Lee said simply, walking over with a dagger at her side. Nadina looked wearily at the dagger then up at her, her head propped up by her hands. "This is torture..." She muttered.

Lee watched her for a moment, then walked to her side and pulled her up. "No. You're not going to give up because you are going to go back to that palace and fight King Latkis! Fight him after all he's ever done to hurt you! After all he's made you do!"

"I thought you didn't believe me about that." Nadina muttered tiredly.

"Well... I don't, but if there's anything that'll get you fighting, it's the thought that you can kick that king's butt, delusional thought or not! And, despite the fact that she was tired beyond all reason, Nadina reluctantly picked up her bow and arrow and went back to work.

Weeks later, Nadina's work really seemed to improve. She could now hit a few inches near the bullseye on nearly every shot she took. She was extremely pleased with herself, but, of course, Lee was not.

"You have to get straight in the bullseye if you ever want to win the fight against Latkis!"

"So that's what this is, then?" The two whipped around to see James standing there, his face blank. Nadina's eyes widened.

"H-how long have you been standing there?" She asked fearfully.

"Long enough." He said sternly. "How could you?! After I literally told you weeks ago you couldn't!"
"And why not?" Nadina asked coldly, her eyes narrowing. "You go out and daringly fight monsters and soldiers! I'm doing this, James- I don't care if you want it or not, because you're NOT mom or dad!" With that, she stormed past him and jumped down the hole to the hideout.

The next few days passed by more slowly than anything either of the twins had ever experienced. Neither were willing to talk to the other, and somehow despite the countless efforts from Reuben and Lee, the two would not utter a word.

Chapter 23

"James! There are two guards up there-" An aging woman ran weakly toward James, who stood up immediately. "Synthia went to get some berries!" She sobbed weakly, shaking uncontrollably. "Y-you have to save her! Th-the guards will kill her if they recognize her from the-" Before she could finish the sentence both James and Nadina sprang up and ran over to the exit/entrance at the same time. They shared a short glare at each other- each daring each other to go first until finally they both clambered up the ladder together, each squished beyond imagination. Miraculously though, they both got above, and just in time, too, for little Synthia was cowering in fear by a tree.

two guards advancing on her. Both twins, strengthened by the others' presence (Though neither was willing to admit it), the two scrambled toward the two trees where they'd hidden spare weapons and took them out- James a dagger and Nadina a bow and arrow. Immediately they took action, and in no time the guards were on the run. But there was one more enemy still not vanquished. A Dilitine- Nadina had discovered the names of a few creatures during her stay- jumped out from behind James and pushed him down. Nadina gasped and held her bow high at the ready, her fingers trembling at the sight of James sprawled across the ground. The Dilitine snarled and pounced at her, then stopped dead and hit the ground with three arrows in its heart. Nadina stood still for a moment, unable to believe her eyes before running over to James, who was sitting up.
"James! Are you okay?!" James looked up after dusting off his shirt, then smiled faintly. "I've seen worse days." Nadina gasped in relief and then flung her arms around him, and the two hugged, their anger long gone.
"Maybe it's best you continue training..." James whispered. "Only I want to teach you."

"Really? Y-you're serious?" She asked, her eyes wide.

"Oh, yeah. I don't want you to become a ruthless murderer like her. Kill of the day? Yikes." He whispered. Nadina laughed, and he leaned closer. "Don't tell her I said that. I don't want to be her kill of the day."

So from then on, Nadina's aim and strength grew more accurate. Each time she was given a target, Nadina was able to hit the bullseye- except for one time when Reuben had accidentally wandered in front of the target, causing Nadina to panic and send the arrow flying toward the sky.

"Okay," Reuben said. "You're ready."

Chapter 24

"To freedom!" Lee yelled in triumph, raising a bottle of wine they had stolen from the castle.

The others cheered- they were all huddled around a small fire in the cave, and though it was dark and damp, they were all grateful to be there.

"To courage!" James yelled out to more cheers.

"To finally getting something good to drink!" Jack- James' friend- yelled to laughter.

Nadina smiled at this, then looked around.
Surrounding her were outcasts, second borns, people she'd have never imagined herself ever being acquainted with.
And yet she couldn't feel more at home.

Chapter 25

"Okay..." Nadina murmured, looking around as she and James walked through the forest. "What are we doing here exactly?"
"We're going to get some allies." He said simply, keeping his gaze forward.
"There are other people living here?"
Her feet were making loud crunchy noises with each step they took.
James rolled his eyes. "No... We're going to see the Lias."
"Which are...?" Nadina asked curiously as she pushed past a hanging branch. The crunching was starting to annoy her.

James was silent for a moment, stopping.
Then he spoke.
"Shape-shifters."
Nadina froze in fear, her blood cold. Suddenly she was aware of their surroundings.
The sky was darker in this part of the forest, making what should have been a bright clearing a dark and spooky part of the forest. The trees were splattered with blood, and when Nadina looked down at the ground on which she was standing on she was horrified to see that she had been stepping on skulls, some half eaten and some with decaying skin still clinging to them. Nadina choked and looked over at James, receiving a shock when she saw that the skulls seemed to have a different effect on him. He was gazing at them wearily, as if he had suddenly grown exhausted and sad. It hurt to see him this way, but what hurt Nadina even more was that she somehow knew that if he weren't there with her, he would have been worse, and the same for herself. She sighed shakily and walked over to him, resting a hand on his arm. He jumped out of his stupor and looked over at her, smiling weakly, and Nadina, with another

pang of sympathy and guilt, realized that he would have broken down right then and there if she wasn't there for him to comfort. She reached out for his hand, and he accepted.
Together they walked, careful so as not to damage the skulls anymore than they already were until, finally, they reached the moss covered cave.
"You okay?" Nadina heard James whisper and jumped to see him looking straight at her. She regained her composure and, silently cursing herself for shaking so much, nodded.
"I'm all right," she said, then added playfully, "and you?"
James smirked and rolled his eyes, looking at the cave.
"I've been here a few times before. This shouldn't be too different."
Nadina raised an eyebrow, but didn't question further. Instead, the two cautiously neared the cave. Nadina looked over at James to see him crouched down, examining a thin black rock. He pressed his thumb down against it, and Nadina suddenly felt a sweeping sensation. The winds changed, as if the world suddenly decided to stand still. The ground suddenly began to shake, then suddenly stopped.

"Hello, Hunter."
Nadina spun around to see James was talking to a dark creature, seeming like black smoke and yet still solid, with thorns coming out of the creature's hooves. Nadina broke into a sweat just looking at the hideous blood red eyes of the monster, and yet she realized that they were the only real part of his body. This must be one of the Lias, she thought. The Lias growled at her, and suddenly Nadina took everything back- she wanted to be at the palace, surrounded by guards and suitors. She'd visit the gossiping maids right before lunch so she could catch up on the latest gossip- perhaps the other kingdom would have forgiven her by now! But then James took her hand in his protectively, and a sense of bravery and safety washed over her. The Lias seemed confused at her sudden lack of fear, as if it had been drinking up every glorious moment of it.
"What are you doing here?" It asked James coldly, turning its gaze to him. As it did, Nadina could feel James freeze. She squeezed his hand gently, and he looked over at her, straightening slightly, then looked over at the Lias. "We need your help."

Chapter 26

"So you want my help to go against the king?" The Lias said in its cold, dreadful voice.
"Yes," James said simply.
Nadina couldn't help but be shocked at his calmness, especially in this situation.
"The last time I helped you we lost Rosaline." The Lias growled. "Why is this situation any different?"

Nadina couldn't help but shiver when the Lias spoke. We? How many more of him were there? Were they in this cave? James gestured toward her, and suddenly she felt scared. What would he say? Was she a sacrifice? She forced herself out of her thoughts and shook her head. James wouldn't do that... Would he?

After all, they had just been reunited... Nadina hadn't even known she had a brother until recently. What made her think she knew so much about him?

"We have her," James said confidently. The Lias looked over at her, and its expression softened ever so slightly. "So you found her?" It mused, then its eyes narrowed. "How do you know this is her?"

"Look at her right arm."

The Lias grunted and walked over to Nadina, who tensed immediately as the air around her seemed to turn sharp. Hairs on the back of her neck stood up, and she looked over at James as if pleading him to stop it, but he only gave her a look of sympathy. She felt as if she were on display. She could hear her heart pounding in her ears as the Lias lifted her arm to

show a long white scar- one she never understood how she got, but always assumed it was from her earlier memories.
"It is her..." The Lias muttered, then looked at James, who nodded. Nadina wanted to roll her eyes and say, yes, it's me! What is the big deal? But she didn't feel that would please the Lias very well. "You're a fool for coming here." The Lias growled. "Especially again, when you left unharmed the last time. Haven't you heard the legend?" This time, James rolled his eyes. "Of course I do. But this is different." He walked over to Nadina and took her hand. "WE'RE different." The Lias made a motion that seemed to have looked like a very rude gesture for humans, but Nadina couldn't be so sure as it only had paws. It inhaled through its' "nose" and its mouth curved into what seemed like a smile. "Ooh, she's a lovely prey." It said in its horrible voice. Nadina felt her blood turn to ice- as if it hadn't already had been. James' grip on her hand tightened, but even his grim face couldn't mask his curiosity.
The Lias stepped forward, and Nadina could hear her heart beating in her ears like a drum.
Thump. Thump. Thump.

Stop. She thought to herself fiercely. All she got in response was a quick piercing pain in her ear, as if her brain were giving her a swift kick in return for her attitude.
"Don't even think about it," James growled. The Lias looked over at him, its gaze narrowing. "You should think twice about what you say to me if you want my help."
"So you're the leader now?"
The Lias' gaze hardened but didn't respond.
"What happened to Skylar?"
"She's still here." It said quietly.
"So... You're not the leader."
It shook his head. James smiled, relieved. Nadina raised an eyebrow. She didn't know who Skylar was, but she knew that she didn't want this... Hunter to be the leader of the pack of Lias.
"Then why are you the one who came out here?" James asked coldly, crossing his arms.
The Lias stayed silent.
"ANSWER ME." James said more loudly. The Lias snarled and pounced at him, but he quickly dodged and drew his

dagger. Nadina gasped. The Lias turned and was about to pounce again when it stopped short and backed away. A girl with dirty blonde hair and deep brown eyes stood by the entrance to the cave, her hand closed in a fist around a necklace around her neck, her other arm raised. Her hand glowed blood red, and her brown eyes livid. Nadina's eyes widened. The girl was beautiful, and yet there was something uneasy about her, but James didn't seem to notice.

"Skylar..." He murmured, his eyes wide.

Skylar looked over at him then stepped forward, glaring at the Lias. "Get in the cave." She growled lowly. The Lias started to protest before she closed her fist again and it scurried off into the cave.

She watched then looked over at James, softening. "Hey." She said softly, putting her hands on her hips. Only then did Nadina notice the state of her clothes. She wore faded pants that were ripped so badly they could have been mistaken for shorts with large hanging threads. Her shirt was gray and torn so it was barely decent, but she didn't seem to notice. Then again, Nadina thought, nobody would really care about the state of their

clothing if they were living in a forest with a bunch of monsters.
"I haven't seen you in a while." She continued.
James nodded, smiling faintly. "Yeah... It's been awhile."
Nadina looked between the two, raising an eyebrow then looked over at Skylar, who, she was shocked to see, was looking back at her. "So... Who's this?" She asked quietly, looking over at James.
"My twin sister." He said softly.
She raised an eyebrow then her eyes widened. "So the prophecy was true then..." She whispered. James nodded, and Nadina raised an eyebrow. "Prophecy?" She started to say, but James muttered, "later." in her ear.
"So what are you two doing here?" Skylar asked, crossing her arms. "I get the feeling this isn't just a catch-up meeting."
James took a moment then nodded. "Yeah... We need your help."

Chapter 27

"So, you gonna tell what that was all about?" Nadina asked quietly, raising an eyebrow. James looked over at her and nodded. They were walking back to the camp, Skylar telling them to wait there before she could give them any further details of their plan. "What was that whole deal with the prophecy?" Nadina asked quietly, looking up at him. James was silent, looking at the ground as he walked. "... When I first was coming to the camp, I met an Ormph." Nadina had heard

of Ormphs before. They were small, delicate creatures who could see glimpses of the future, but they'd only tell anyone in prophecy form to mess with their heads.
"And?" She asked quietly, looking over at him. He stopped walking and looked over at her, then took a deep breath before speaking.

"Child of betrayal,
Consumed by dark,
Shall destroy the love of hearts.
Overrun by fear and need,
The throne's cruel orders the child shall heed."

Nadina was too stunned to speak.
James looked over at her and sighed. "We're children of betrayal, Nadina. Our parents disobeyed king Latkis, they betrayed his rules." Nadina looked down, concentrating hard. "And... And the love of all hearts?" She asked quietly. "True love," James whispered, looking back down. "All I can think of to fit the description is that." Nadina nodded, though she didn't

want to admit it. They were now passing a spot in the forest- well, not really a forest- where there were no trees or grass at all. Not a single sign of life.

"James...?" She asked quietly, stopping for a moment.

James stopped and looked around, then shook his head. "It was probably a forest fire."

"Then what put it out before it got to the rest?" She asked, but he didn't respond. She didn't mind, though, as there was something else on her mind.

As James had told her the prophecy, a sudden name had sprung into her mind- Dillan. She didn't remember what he looked like exactly, but she knew that the feelings she'd experienced with him were something outside of friendship. She sighed and closed her eyes, hugging herself tightly. Both of them had lovers. She had seen enough of the way James and Skylar looked at each other to know that they were in love, although she wasn't sure of herself and Dillan being in love. Was she going to hurt James? She'd never! But as she thought about it, she realized how she hadn't particularly enjoyed Skylar's presence when they first met. At the time she thought it was because of her being a half-Lias, but now she realized it was because she had just found James, and already he was in love with someone. What else had she missed? He was her twin brother, and it bothered her that it didn't seem like they were related at all, despite the energy bursts they seemed to get whenever they were around each other. She sighed and looked down. "... It can be either of us." She whispered. James nodded and looked down, probably thinking of Skylar, and Nadina couldn't help but think that James could do the same to her with Dillan... That is, if they were true love. She didn't know, but she'd always hoped to have a relationship like the ones in stories she'd read in the books she was dusting in the castle. She snapped out of her daze when they reached the camp. Then she realized- all these people had loved ones in their lives. She could destroy any one of these people's lives. She shivered then looked down. She'd lose the sliver of respect that Lee possibly had for her. And Reuben? He'd saved her from Lee's wrath. How would he react when she betrayed his trust- and destroyed the love of someone's life. She jumped down the hole after James, watched the circular door of the tree move back

into place, moved to her corner, sat, and began to think about the prophecy, but her eyelids became too heavy, and soon enough she fell asleep. All too soon, she woke up to the sound of a girl her age running past her. "James!" She yelled out. Nadina wondered stupidly, how does she know James? When she realized EVERYONE here knew James. He was their leader. Again, she felt upset. She had missed WAY too much in her brother's life, and she was NOT going to continue missing out. She got up and ran after the girl to see her in James' room, walking over to James, who raised an eyebrow.
"Daphne... What is it?"
"I have news..." Daphne said breathlessly. "From the castle."
Immediately, James straightened, and Nadina raised an eyebrow. How could this Daphne know what was going on in the castle? They were way too deep in the forest to have any communication with the village, let alone the kingdom.
"What news?" James asked. Even though the tone of his voice was calm, Nadina could read right through it to the eagerness. She could understand why. Any type of news from the world

outside the forest would be amazing right now, when they were so secluded. Nadina would even settle for the maid's gossip. But Daphne didn't have that in mind. She put up her hands as if in defense, then slowly dropped them then moved them to the side. As she did, the winds seemed to follow her motions until they became visible- a beautiful mixture of colors so various that Nadina's human mind couldn't grasp it- all she could do was stare at the colors, but that wasn't the right word for them. The colors didn't deserve to be tied down by a simple word. They were bright, but not too bright- a mixture of all the colors ever tied into one, glittering wind. Nadina wasn't shocked to find herself gaping. They were gone too soon, forming into an image of a room in the castle, a room she only recognized from the descriptions some lucky maids had described to her. The room was pale yellow, with a bright canopy bed in the right corner of it. The walls were decorated by what would have been the most beautiful paintings Nadina had ever seen, if she hadn't had seen the wind's true color just a moment ago. This was the Queen Ariana's room, which had never been cleaned out, and the king sat on his knees by the bed, his head down. "Ariana..." He whispered, looking up, and Nadina was shocked to see that his face was contorted with sorrow and agony. She was also surprised that she felt a little sorry for him. This guy had ruined her life, yet she couldn't help but feel sorry for him. She shook her head as a man– Olmer, the royal sorcerer– walked into the room, lingering at the doorway.

"Your majesty." He said quietly, bowing. The king looked up at him, raising an eyebrow. "Don't try to rub it in, Olmer." He growled.

The sorcerer put up his hands in defense. "I just came here to tell you– you need to take action. The prophecy is bound to come true soon." The king's eyes narrowed. "The prophecy killed my family, Olmer. I will not listen to any more of this nonsense." Olmer glared at him then looked down. "Because you always ignore the prophecies! That's why your wife and daughter died!"

The King's eyes widened. Nadina felt like she wanted to shrink from the way the king was glaring at Olmer.

There was silence for what seemed like hours.

"Tell me the prophecy." He said coldly, his eyes still sad yet boring into Olmer.
"I already told you it." He said simply.
The king raised an eyebrow, then let his eyes narrow. "I told you I wasn't interested in that." He said sternly.
"And look where that got you." Olmer said coldly. "Your daughter's dead, and the twins have escaped!"
The king growled. "Do not question my motives."
Olmer stared at him then shook his head. "You are so ignorant." He whispered. "These children will be your doom. Arbia confirms this."
"And what do you care of the old buffoon's say in the matter?" The king scoffed, and Nadina felt a twinge of pain in her chest, as if the king had poked her with a sharp stick. She put a hand to her chest, then felt the pain die away and lowered it.
"He still taught me, your majesty." Olmer muttered, his round face red as a beet.
"Yes, and you left him– the right thing to do I must add."
"Thank you, your majesty."

The king nodded then turned away from him. "How can I stop them? I've already separated them as babies."
Olmer rolled his eyes. "And that got you... Where?"
The King stayed silent, then shook his head. "So tell me how to fix it!"
Olmer started to speak, but suddenly the image got fuzzy and vanished. Daphne fell to the floor, but not before James caught her. She groaned, opening her eyes slightly and looking around the room, hesitantly placing a hand on her forehead. "Wh-where am I?" She asked weakly. Nadina stared at her then looked up at James, her eyes wide.
"This has happened before." He reassured her quickly, then looked back down at Daphne. "You're in the camp, and you just gave a prophecy."
Daphne's eyes widened, but it seemed like she understood.
Nadina stared at Daphne's unusually gray eyes, and for a moment she thought she could see those colors again.
Nadina looked up at James. "Hey, um... Can we talk?"
James raised an eyebrow before nodding. "Sure. Uh- Daphne, could you-?"

Daphne nodded and hurried out of the room, leaving the twins.
"So... You have a prophet..." She said quietly, looking up at him. "How did I not notice that over the past few weeks?"
"Daphne only gets these things once or twice a month." He replied, looking ahead of him. Nadina couldn't help but realize how much he looked like a soldier, standing straight and tall with his muscles profound.
"And... What's the deal with Skylar?"
He stopped short from pacing and looked over at her, probably thinking of the prophecy, Nadina realized, then looked down.
"... I love her." He whispered, staring at the hard floor.
"But she's a Lias." She whispered. Even as she said the words and knew she believed in them, it pained her to disagree with her brother– her twin– being happy.
"She's a half Lias." James snapped quickly, then sighed and ran his hands through his hair.
"But do you really think you can trust her? That she'll help us?" Nadina asked, her voice barely audible in her fear of being snapped at again.

"... Yes." James said quietly, taking a moment before looking up at her. "Look, I know she doesn't seem... Very nice from what you saw." Nadina's mind instantly went to an image of the Lias Hunter cowering in fear before her, "but she has an amazing heart... And I don't love the fact that she may be able to help us. I love her– and if you loved someone then you'd know how I feel right now, and be on my side!"

Nadina hung her head, closing her eyes. James raised an eyebrow, then let his eyes widen. "What... Do you feel that way towards someone?"

Nadina took a moment then looked down. "Not exactly..."

James raised an eyebrow.

"I love someone like a sibling." Nadina whispered, looking up at him. James raised an eyebrow, taking a moment before grinning that dazzling grin of his.

"We must be twins, because I've got the same feeling."

Nadina looked up at him, then ran over and hugged him tightly, shutting her eyes. James closed his eye as well, holding her close to him.

Nadina had left something out, though. As she spoke with James, her mind had wandered back to a particular guard miles away from them at the palace, who stood guard in the dungeons at times and had saved her life... And as she thought back to him the name sprang to the front of her mind.

Dillan.

Did she love him? Did she truly know what love was? How could she be so sure that this was what she thought it was? How could she know that Dillan felt the same way? How could she know if Dillan was still alive? Maybe he was dead already, punished by the king for helping her escape...

She shuddered. She hated to think of it- was that a sign of love? Was that a sign of... anything?

James pulled away and nodded. "Okay... Now let's-"

Suddenly Lee ran in, her dagger out in her hand and gasping for breath.

"Guards- outside- hurry up!"

James quickly unsheathed his sword he had won in a battle against some stray guards and hurried out of the room, Nadina right behind him.

Reuben was outside, fighting five guards at once and severely losing. Lee ran up to one from behind and tapped the guard on the shoulder. The guard spun around, and Lee clashed her dagger against his sword, making a brilliant clank. James ran up to one of the guards and rolled by his feet, standing up and getting into a sword fight with the guard. Another dark skinned boy around age seventeen or so was already in an intense fight with a tall guard who seemed more trained than all the others combined. Nadina gasped as a guard began to run towards the direction of the castle and swung- the dagger Lee had given her just barely missed him and she realized- they were all just kids. Lee, Reuben, James and her- they were running an entire resistance- and they weren't even of age! She clashed her dagger against the smooth surface of the guard's sword, sparks flying. If her parents had been alive right then- would they have been proud? Would they have approved? She ducked as the guard swung and tried for a swing at his stomach, but he dodged and clashed his sword against her dagger. Nadina, using all her might to keep the sword from pushing down her dagger, and hoping that her foot wouldn't

slip, realized that it was because of her that her parents were dead in the first place. If they were alive right then, they wouldn't have this to judge- they could be living happily at their cottage with James bringing home Skylar to their approval, celebrating holidays together and singing songs- either way she wouldn't be a part of any of that alternate universe- because it didn't exist- not for her.
She suddenly realized there was a lesser tone to the clashing of swords and daggers and snapped out of her daze- the guard she had been fighting had taken advantage of her daze and vanished. She gasped and ran after him, but he was out of sight.
Later, as Lee went on yelling about how much Nadina had cost them, James stepped forward and said two words, to the entire camp.
"It's time."

Chapter 28

It was her fault. That was all that Nadina could think as they trudged through the mud to the Lias' cave. If it hadn't been for her, it might have been years before they'd have to come here again or to fight at all.

But that wasn't the only thing. It was her fault that James wasn't happy right now, with their parents in a warm cottage without ever having to worry about prophecies or powers or anything.

She watched James walk, and wondered what he thought of the matter. What could he think, besides it being her fault her all his pain? If she hadn't been born he could have been happy.

-*-

They reached the cave, and James picked up the black rock, feeling its smooth surface before looking up. Skylar stood before them, and for a moment Nadina could see how James was in love with her. At one moment her hair was scraggly and dead from all the years with the Lias, but the next moment she was beautiful- liven up to her full potential. Her dirty blonde hair was smooth and fell gracefully down her shoulders, her clothing was whole and clean, and her eyes- well, not much changed in them except the light in them.

"Skylar," James said quietly, stepping forward. As he did, the form of her true potential faded from Nadina's eyes, and she looked over at James.

"We need your answer- now. Can you or can you not get the Lias to help us with the rebellion?"

"Of course." Skylar replied simply, her fingers trailing over the necklace around her neck.
James eyed it a little uneasily, then looked back up at her.
"And... How soon can you get them to help?"
"As soon as you like."
James took a moment, then nodded. "Good. Have them all ready tomorrow at dawn."
Skylar nodded, then looked down. "... I'll see you then." She whispered. Nadina watched, then realized with shock Skylar was scared. She didn't want to risk their lives.
James seemed to notice this, too, because he stepped forward, then looked over at Nadina, who nodded immediately and walked away into the forest.
James watched then looked over at Skylar, who kept her gaze down.
"We're gonna be okay..." He started to say, but Skylar cut him off.
"No, we're not." She whispered, looking up at him. "Even if we survive this, I'm still a monster to anyone who sees me beside you and the other Lias! They'll never see me for my human side.

only for my Lias side." Her eyes were pained, and it killed James to see her like that. He wanted to make her feel better, to cure those beautiful brown eyes so that she could be happy again.
"But I see you for your human side." He whispered, then looked down. "And who wants to be human anyway? Humans are full of mistakes!" He exclaimed, looking around. "We're all about war, and we say we want peace but how do we get that? Oh, that's right! War!" He lifted her chin up, and she looked up at him.
"The point is, I love you, whether you're a Lias or a human. Because we're all full of mistakes." He whispered softly, before pressing his lips against hers gently. Skylar took a moment before closing her eyes and wrapping her arms around him.
"I love you too..." She whispered.
Nadina watched from the forest then looked down at the bones of human bodies. Had Skylar done any of that? Would James become one of those decayed bodies? She shuddered to think of it, then looked down and shut her eyes tightly. James walked over, raising an eyebrow.

"Hey... You okay?"
Nadina looked up and nodded quickly. "Oh- yeah. I'm okay... Just a bit nervous..." She said weakly, looking back down.
"Well, don't be... You've had weeks of train-"
"Weeks!" Nadina exclaimed weakly, looking up at him. "And how many have you had? A week more than I had? We're just beginners, James! We have almost no experience in battle, and now we're going to war?! We're not ready for this!"
"We have to act now!" James said, his eyes wide. "That guard knows the whereabouts of the camp. We'd be endangering the lives of almost a hundred people down there! And do you think the king will stop there?! Of course, not! He will continue to search for any sympathizer or villager that goes one step out of line and kill or torture them on the spot! He is not like us, Nadina! We have to take him down!"
Nadina felt tears sting at the back of her eyes, then bit her lip. James stared at her, then looked down.
"He killed our parents, Nadina. Doesn't that mean anything-?"
"Of course it does!" Nadina yell. "It means he's a monster, but we can't kill him-"

"You think our parents were the only ones?!" James asked in shock, his eyes wide. "They weren't even the start of things!"
"Lee's dad left her mom pregnant and sentenced to execution, Nadina, almost about the same time our parents were killed! And that's not even the start of it!"
"Janelle's mother is mute, she used to work in the castle just like us but was banished after having twins."
"Twins?" Nadina asked, raising an eyebrow. "What do you mean twins? I thought Janelle was an only child."
"Well, she wasn't. The king found out and had the boy executed."
Nadina blinked. That could have been them. That so easily could have been them, and yet it wasn't. Their parents stood in the way, all because of her. She had no time to finish the thought, though, as James wasn't finished.
"Reuben doesn't even have a family, and yet he's still here to help the unfortunate people that were affected by the king! He doesn't know anything about himself because of the king's rules! All he knows is that he wants to help these people–"
and Lee, Nadina thought.

"Then there's Tom, whose dad was killed for lying to the king. Jackson, who Reuben only just found last month tortured, Sara–"

"Okay, I get it!" Nadina exclaimed, tears trickling down her cheeks. "You don't have to express it anymore. I get it!" She took a shaky breath then shook her head, sniffing before turning and running off.

Chapter 29

She had no destination, no hope to find anyone or anything. She just wanted to put distance between herself and James.

She pushed away a loose branch that scratched at her face and continued running before feeling a large amount of mass fall upon her, tackling her to the ground. She gasped and looked up. A Lias stood before her, growling lowly in hunger.

She stared at it then slowly took a step back, gulping. The Lias growled, then slowly a gray mist swirled around it, completely covering it. Suddenly the mist subsided.

Nadina squinted, then let her eyes widen at the person before her.

Dillan stepped forward, a soft smile on his lips. "Hey."
Nadina gulped and quickly shook her head, taking a step back.
"Nadina, it's me." Dillan said worriedly, staring at her.
"No- no, it isn't! Y-you're a Lias!" She cried out.
He raised an eyebrow, then shook his head. "No, I'm not..."
Nadina shook her head, hearing the magic persuasion in his voice and deflecting it as much as she could, but a small part of her wanted to listen to it.
Dillan took another step forward, but not before he gasped and shrank into a small amount of mist. James stepped out from behind him, his eyes narrowed in anger as he sheathed his dagger.
"James-" Nadina started, but burst into tears.
James stared at her then sighed and looked down, shaking his head.
"Look, I'm- I'm sorry that I got mad before." James muttered. "I-I know how hard it probably is... To be a maid, and then suddenly going through a big change like that-"
Nadina shook her head and ran over, hugging him tightly.

"I don't care... I don't care..." She whispered, burying her face into his shoulder. "Let's just- let's just get it over with..."
"YES!"
Nadina jumped and looked over at Lee, who stood with her arms crossed, grinning.
"Why are you so happy?" James asked, pulling away and looking over at her.
Lee shrugged. "Because," she said, a mischievous look in her eyes. "This means we can finally start the war."

Chapter 30

"Ready?" James asked, raising his sword by its hilt.

Nadina hesitated, looking up at the castle looming over them.

"No turning back." Reuben muttered, taking out an arrow and resting it against his bow string.

Lee watched then put a hand on the dagger in her belt, her eyes scanning the castle.

Nadina took this all in through fearful eyes, though the fear was well hidden.

James glanced her way and smiled faintly– a sign of encouragement that sent warmth coursing through her body.

shielding her against the cold. She smiled back as best as she could and took her bow from across her chest, careful as not to disturb her sword.

She nodded slightly at James, who returned the gesture and raised his hand, whistling two flat keys, then one high note.

Instantly, there was an explosion, and the drawbridge to the castle came crashing down, landing in front of them.

There was silence for a moment, then one of the Lias in the back let out a howl–

And the fight was on.

Nadina looked around as all the rebels ran into the castle, their weapons raised and arrows flying.

Her breaths were coming in sharply, and all around her was a blur.

She closed her eyes and shook her head for a moment, calming herself down before opening her eyes, narrowly avoiding crashing into a snarling Lias then turned toward the castle and ran in, looking around.

She could feel the adrenaline pulsing through her veins, her training kicking in.

She stopped running when she spotted a guard, becoming more silent and hiding behind a pillar.
She peeked out from behind it and raised her bow, pulling back the arrow. She had spent weeks training in target practice and fencing, stealth and silence.
But was she ready to kill?
She didn't know.
Maybe she could hit him somewhere it wouldn't kill him...
Her fingers burned against the bowstring, begging her to release it. She suppressed a whimper and let go, not aiming for a specific spot as her fingers burned too much for her to try.
The arrow flew across the room and stabbed into the guard's fifth rib, instantly killing him.
There was no howl of pain. There was no final wish.
All that sounded in the hall was the crash of metal as the guard's once living body fell into a suit of armor, and the distant clashes of swords.
Nadina stood frozen, unable to process what should have been clear.
She'd killed him.

She, Nadina- who could never hurt a fly- had sent an arrow string straight through that man's heart.
Then a horrible thought struck her- what if this man had a family?
A wife, standing by the door of their cottage, eagerly waiting to say the following- "How was your day? Oh, I'm so glad you're home!"
She choked on a sob and then looked down at the man.
There was no turning back from this.
She took a deep breath and closed her eyes, trying to imagine this man as one of the practice dummies from the camp.
She had just succeeded in making a target seem to appear on the man's chest when another guard ran into the hall.
She gasped and grabbed an arrow, the arrow at the ready in an instant.
The guard stopped short, his eyes wide.

"Nadina?"

Chapter 31

Nadina stared, too shocked to speak, at the guard who had saved her life- and who she now had to kill.
She steadied her breathing, and her training kicked back in.
She raised her bow.
Dillan stared at her then let out a nervous laugh, stepping forward.
"Come on, Nadina. You wouldn't shoot."
Nadina felt tears stinging at the back of her eyes.

She loved him. She knew that. Even back in the camp when she'd been questioning the fact, in the back of her mind she had known she loved him.

So why was it so hard to put down the bow? Maybe it wasn't. Maybe this was all a delusion, perhaps she just wanted to think she could be tough, when all she'd been doing was ensuring that there'd be no chance of a happy ending for her and Dillan.

Shall destroy the love of hearts.

She took a deep breath, blinked back her tears, and let the arrow loose.

Dillan's eyes widened, but not before the arrow whizzed inches past his right ear and hit the advancing guard behind him.

Dillan spun around and looked down at the whimpering guard on the floor, who was covered in blood. He continued to flail around on the ground for a few moments then lay still, unconscious.

Dillan turned around to see, to his relief, that Nadina's bow was hanging across her chest again, but was shocked to see her drawing her sword.

"Nadina- what are you-?"

"I saved your life." She said, and was surprised to hear how much her voice had grown from a gentle maid's to a fierce warrior's, but it was the same voice, just with a little more ferocity.
"Now we're even, and we duel." She whispered.
Dillan took a moment, then drew his sword as well, a worried look in his eyes.
"Are you sure you want to do this?" He asked quietly, raising an eyebrow. "I-I do have more experience..."
Nadina let her eyes narrow. What was that supposed to mean?
"Yes." She said quietly, stepping forward. Dillan took a moment, then thrust his sword forward, Nadina parrying before advancing.
"So- I see you've gotten better." He said as he continued to advance.
"How would you know? You've never even dueled me before."
"Well, now I know that you're good." He replied.
She smiled faintly in spite of herself- it was impossible for her not to, despite the short amount of time they had known each other for.

She swung her sword, gasping when she almost hit him, but he parried and stepped forward.
"Where have you been, Nadina?" He whispered as she tried to swing.
"In the magical land where people can have more than one child." She said, her tone getting stern for reasons she did not know.
He raised an eyebrow, then shrugged, continuing to parry as she swung harder and harder, the anger she had been holding in suddenly spilling out.
"Woah!" Dillan shouted, staring at her as she got into full mode. "Nadina, calm down!"
"You do realize this is a serious duel, right? We're enemies. We're not just practicing!"
He stopped for a moment, and Nadina, seizing the opportunity, lunged forward and stopped just as the tip of her sword was about to hit his chest. He looked down at the flat of her sword against his chest then looked up at her, sadness in his eyes.
"You really believe we're enemies?"

She raised an eyebrow. What else was she supposed to believe? He was a guard for the king, a king who had killed and hurt many people, a lot of which she had just recently come to known.
But– he did save her, and she knew they had some sort of connection... Maybe he wasn't bad?
But then why would he still be working for the king? And helping him destroy thousands of people's lives?
"I don't approve of his motives, Nadina." He said quietly, as if reading her thoughts. "I'm doing this for my family–"
"Your family?" She asked weakly, looking up at him. "Let me paint a picture for you, Dillan."
He winced at the sound of her saying his name, as if he'd imagined her say it before but not in this tone of voice.
"What if your mother– right now– was brought into the castle because she had a second child? What if she was about to be killed?"
He stared at her then looked down, muttering something she couldn't hear.

She shook her head in disappointment, turning away. "Goodbye, Dillan." She whispered, tears stinging in the back of her eyes as she walked away.

Chapter 32

Lee walked down the hall, her hand on the dagger in her belt, her eyes narrowed on the hallway before her.

She was filled with rage and desire– desire for revenge on the king and all the suffering he had caused her and her family.

She continued down the hall, her thoughts filled with memories– and those memories filled with pain.

Suddenly there was a crash nearby, and she jumped at the sudden sound, whipping out her dagger.

The king hurried her way, then stopped and his eyes widened. There he was. All she had to do was kill him, right there and then. Her fingers tapped against the handle of the dagger

restlessly, sweating from her tight grip she had been using just moments before.
The two stared at each other for a moment before the king came out of his shock and turned around, running the other way.
Lee didn't have to tell herself twice to run after him, heck, she didn't have to say it once. Her legs were already running at top speed after him, her eyes narrowed on her target.
She could easily shoot him with an arrow- but she'd given her bow to Reuben- he was a better shot than her.
Dang it.
She could throw her dagger at him, but then it would be stained with his filthy blood, and she did not want that beast's blood on her prized possession.
She had a few small contraptions from Eka, who had supplied them with most of their weapons.
Lee handled her dagger.
Plus, it had been her father's.
King Latkis ran into the throne room, shutting the doors quickly.
A guard saw him running and stepped in front of the doors protectively.

Knowing there were no other doors to let the king out, Lee stopped, satisfied that her prey was trapped- right where he belonged. She smiled sweetly as she neared the guard and hid her dagger behind her back. The guard looked down at her, slight confusion entering his eyes.
"Hello." She said cheerfully. "Sorry to bother you, but my friend Mr. king is in there, and we were scheduled for a little playdate at about..." She looked at an imaginary watch on her wrist, then looked up at him. "Three years ago."
The guard started to speak when she cocked her head to the side. "No? Well, I guess I'll just be going then." She said quietly, taking out her dagger. "Or you will."
She cut into his leg and he cried out, falling to the floor.
She looked down at him, already in a puddle of his own blood in those few seconds before she opened the door and shut it behind her, looking over at the terrified king in the corner of the room.
"This is long overdue." She whispered, starting to walk over to him.
"Wait!" He cried out.
She didn't. She continued advancing on him.

"Y-your friend! He's in danger!" He cried.
Her eyes narrowed, but her thoughts jumped to Reuben.
"Nice try."
"It's not a try!" He said desperately. "Your friend is in danger!"
"And why would you care?"
"Because it'll at least prevent you from killing me." He said simply.
She stared at him then looked down. He was right. She had to know if Reuben was okay.
"How is he in danger?" She asked sternly, glaring down at him.
"The Lias." He said simply. "That girl."
She took a moment, then her eyes widened. "Skylar? Sh-she wouldn't."
"You don't seem to be so confident about that."
She stared at him then looked down. Was Skylar trustworthy? She had never met the Lias, and... Well, she was a half Lias! But James trusted her... Maybe even loved her.
But she loved Reuben.

She sighed and stood up, glaring at the king. "I'll deal with you later." She growled, turning to see Nadina. Just in time.
"Hold him!" She managed to tell as she ran past.
Nadina watched then looked at the king, who sighed and shut his eyes.
"You deserve to die, you know." She whispered.
He didn't respond.
"After everything you've done, after all the torture and pain you've inflicted, you still won't admit it?" She asked in disbelief, then scoffed. "You're a monster-"
"Then why don't you kill me?" He growled, glaring up at her. "Why don't you just end this now, and kill me?! I'm the last of the royals. I'm the last of my family! Everyone else is dead! So let me be with them!"
Nadina stood up. "That's your punishment, your majesty." She said quietly. "You'll just have to wait."
She turned and walked out the door, looking over at Jack, a fellow rebel and nodded at the door. "The king's in there, guard him."

He nodded and started to go in, but she stopped him. "Don't lay a finger on him."

Jack nodded, upset, but he nevertheless obeyed and went into the room.

Nadina nodded, then turned and ran down the hall.

Lee looked around then ran down the hall, stomping her foot in frustration. Where was she?

It took a whole search of the castle before she found Skylar and James out in the courtyard, both fighting a handful of guards.

She took a moment, then sighed. Skylar was amazing at fighting, parrying and swinging her sword at just the right times. Lee could tell she was using her Lias strength by the inhuman power she was using to clash her sword against the guards.

James was doing almost just as well, but his swings could never compare to the power of a half Lias.

She was a great ally to them, and would probably be missed.

But Reuben was in danger because of her.
Maybe she could distract her?
She took a moment, then took out a small circular object- a stringer, which was a small distraction that would latch onto one person.
Would it work on a Lias?
She took a moment then took it out, moving her thumb across its round surface.
She looked over her shoulder at an advancing guard and throwing a small knife into his stomach.
She didn't have time for another guard.
It was worth it for Reuben, she decided, and threw the strinter at Skylar, who turned around just in time to see it coming.
She caught it and dropped it just as it let out a small puff of smoke. Lee dropped her face into her hand. She'd failed.
Skylar continued fighting, but the strinter slowly started beeping and she turned around, distracted by the high pitched sound, only audible to her.

-*-

Reuben ran down the hall, hiding from view when he saw a guard. He had injured a guard around a half hour ago, and he was not going to experience the pain that followed again. He waited a few moments for the guard to go down the hall before running outside. He had to make sure Lee was okay.

He ran out to the courtyard to see Lee with her hand on James' shoulder, her head down.

James was knelt by Skylar's lifeless body, his face covered in trails of tears.

It only took a moment for him to realize what had happened and ran over.

"James..." Lee whispered, staring at him. "We can't stay here."

James shook his head, gasping for air as he cried out. "I can't leave her!" Reuben watched, his eyes wide. He had never seen his friend in so much pain.

"Skylar..." James moaned, shutting his eyes tightly.

Lee watched, closing her eyes.

Reuben didn't know what to do, but his thoughts were interrupted as Nadina ran into view

with an elderly man, panting as she impatiently knocked a guard in her way unconscious.
"I got him." She panted out.
Lee stood up quickly, running over and leaving a confused Reuben to console James.
"Where is she?" The old man asked, his voice soft and sad.
"Right here." Nadina whispered, looking over at him.
The man nodded and kneeled down, feeling Skylar's forehead and then her pulse.
"What are you doing, idiot? She's dead!" James screamed, his eyes suddenly filled with anger.
"I just had to check..." He murmured.
"What is he doing here, anyway?!" James yelled angrily, glaring at Nadina, whose eyes filled with shock and hurt.
"I... I just brought him here to see if he could help."
"SHE'S DEAD!" He screamed out, clutching Skylar's lifeless body as if it were the only thing keeping him alive. "Who do you think you are?!" He yelled at the man.
"James..." Nadina whispered softly. "This is Arbia, he wants to help."

"I DON'T CARE!" He screamed, his eyes bloodshot and his face tight. "Unless he has some sort of healing powers, he CAN'T help!"
"But he does have powers." She said softly. "He's a sorcerer."
James shook his head, showing no sign that he'd heard any of this.
The man, Arbia, knelt down beside James, putting his hand on his shoulder.
Reuben tore his eyes away from James to look at Lee, who seemed to be troubled. What was she thinking about?
"Fine." James muttered, keeping his gaze away from the sorcerer.
Arbia took a moment then looked down. "So... You'd do anything to get her back?"
"Yes." James said through gritted teeth.
"Then you need to make a sacrifice."
"A what?"
Arbia sighed, looking over at him. "A sacrifice. Bringing back the dead has been impossible for many, many years, but this girl–"

"Skylar." James growled.
"–Skylar." He continued. "She just recently died. It may be possible to bring her back, but only if..."
Lee looked up. "Only if someone goes instead."
James looked over at her and Nadina quickly shook her head. "No. There is no way anyone is giving up their lives!"
Reuben glared up at Arbia. "We'd just be trading lives?! How is that fair?"
"It isn't."
James took a moment then looked down. "It... It would be better if she was alive... Instead of me..."
Nadina looked around at him quickly. "What?! No! Nobody is dying!"
"Except for Skylar, but no, wait, she's already dead!" He said impatiently as Lee quickly jabbed a coming guard in the stomach. "I can't live with myself knowing I'd passed up the chance to bring her back!"
"And I won't be able to live without my brother!" She yelled angrily, tears entering her eyes. "I'd just found you a few

months ago! I'm not ready to lose you again!" She choked on a sob and looked away, shutting her eyes tightly.

Reuben watched sadly then looked down.

James stared at her. He had no idea he'd meant so much to her, and he knew he would never want to lose her. But... He couldn't pass up saving Skylar...

"James." Nadina took a shaky breath. "I-I understand how much you love her... B-but think about how many people are going to miss you... And either way, you wouldn't be able to be with her! Hear me out..."

James stared at her then looked down. "I-I don't know what to do..." He whispered. He looked over at Skylar's lifeless face, stroking her cheek gently. He then looked up at Nadina, a tear sliding down his cheek. "... I want her to live."

She nodded sadly and turned away.

She closed her eyes tightly, but it was too late. Tears slid down her cheeks and fell to the ground, leaving dark smudges in the dirt.

James looked over at Arbia. "I-I'll do it."

He nodded and stepped back, picking up his hands. A purplish glow appeared, black creeping along the inside of it and white on the out. James looked down at it warily, sighing before looking up at Arbia and stepping forward, but not before Lee pulled him back.
"James, you need to think about this." She said sternly, but he pulled away.
"There's nothing to think about." He looked over his shoulder at Arbia. "I'm doing this."
"No." Lee grabbed his chin and forced him to look her way. "You're going to listen to me, and you're going to listen good. This is your life you're giving up!"
"So that Skylar can have hers. I love her."
"Well, you won't be with her if you give up your life!" She insisted angrily. "You'll always be apart from her!"
He stared at her, then a look of realization entered his face.
"... You're right."
"Either way, you're never going to be with her, you might as well– did you say I'm right?"

"Yeah." James said quietly, looking down. "If I give up my life for hers, we'll just be miserable without each other... But we need a sacrifice to bring her back... What was it you were saying?" He looked up at Lee, who froze.
"Uh... I-I can't seem to remember."
"Something about I might as well do something? Give me advice, then. Tell me."
"No." She said sternly.
He drew back, a stony look on his face. "If we can't be together in life, then we'll be together in death." He looked down at a dagger on the floor, picking it up and about to turn it towards himself when a rock came out of nowhere, hitting the dagger out of his grasp.
Nadina came into view, her face emotionless yet trails of tears were fresh on her cheeks. "Don't you dare." She growled.
James stared at her. "Excuse me?"
"I said, don't you dare."
"You can't tell me what I can or can't do."
"No, but I can stop you."

"It's my choice." He growled, bending to pick up the dagger when Reuben pushed him against a tree, out of grasp of the dagger.
"James, you need to think about this! There's no going back from it!"
James glared at him, his eyes filled with tears before he looked away.
Lee stepped up to him. "James... This choice is permanent. You have to think about this. To rush into it is just- it's insane!"
"It's my choice." He repeated, then looked up at them. "You don't understand how she was... She was always so... so calm. She knew what to do all the time, and she was..."
"Indescribable."
James looked over at the sound, his eyes finding Nadina, who stepped forward.
"James, I can't say I know how you feel, but right now I think I'm pretty close to it. I just found you, I don't want to lose you... I-I can't lose you." She whispered, choking on her tears. "I want you to be happy, I do! I just... I want to be happy with you... I c-can't lose you!" She cried out, staring at him.

James stared at her, his tearful glare slowly breaking away.
"I'm still learning about the world, about you, about everything!" She continued. "You're all I really have! But if you want to trade that for death, so you can be with your true love," She stopped and looked down. "I understand."
She shut her eyes tightly, tears sliding down her cheeks onto the ground. She tried to shut out the footsteps, most likely of her brother leaving her, but suddenly she felt his arms around her, the warmth of her brother filling her against the terrible cold she was feeling.
She let out a sob, crying with her brother as they embraced each other like they never did before, and the short months they'd had together flashed before them.
After what was too short a time they pulled away from each other, still holding on.
"I have to let go." James whispered, filled with sadness.
Nadina shook her head quickly, crying still. "No... No... P-please, don't go..." She cried weakly.
He tried to smile, but it was a feeble attempt that failed. "I love you." He whispered.

"I love you too."

He sighed shakily, then slowly pulled away, and she felt as if he were ripping out her heart with every step he took away from her.

"W-wait!" She cried out.

He turned around.

"You shouldn't d-die by your own hands... You need to die in battle... So y-you can die protecting others..."

He took a moment then nodded. "You're right."

She held out her hand for him to take. "So... Will you have your last battle with me, brother?"

He smiled weakly and nodded, taking her hand. "I will."

And together they went.

A Last Chapter

Nadina sat by the white tombstone closest to the forest, resting by the front of it Gladioli.
She sniffed, nodding slightly before standing slowly.
"Nadina." Lee whispered, resting her hand on her shoulder.
She looked at her gratefully. Lee had come to her a few hours ago in tears, telling her how she was responsible for Skylar's death, but she understood.
It was king Latkis's work.

For all the times she had thought Lee was a ruthless, heartless killer she smiled back on that thought. Lee had changed so much. So had she.
She looked over her shoulder to see Dillan staring sadly at the grave, careful not to look her in the eye. He had a cut in the shape of an x, the symbol of a traitor guard, on his arm.
Reuben walked over to her. "We need to decide who'll take over the kingship." He whispered. "James would have wanted it over with."
She nodded. She knew he would have.
"I nominate Nadina Orlan for the position of queen of Saffa."
Nadina's eyes widened as she looked over at Janelle, who smiled faintly at her, her beautiful eyes filled with sadness.
"I second that."
Daphne nodded at her.
Around the small crowd there were nods and hands raised, sending warmth to Nadina.
"It's settled then." Lee said quietly, looking over at Nadina. "Your highness."
Nadina tried to smile, but stopped. This wasn't her destiny.

"Thank you, all of you, but I have to resign my post. This is not who I'm meant to be. I want to give you all happiness, the happiness that you should have had long ago, the happiness my brother should have had. I appoint Dillan, a man who had been fighting blindly for what he believed to be good almost all his life, but turned to our side when he saw our cause. He is one of the many reasons we have won this war, and so I appoint him king."

The crowd applauded him, even though they did not know who he was. Even though he had been on the other side. He had helped them, he was with them, he would lead them.

Reuben led him to Nadina, where he hugged her gently.

"Now we're even." Nadina whispered playfully into his ear, a smile in her tone.

He pulled away and stared at her, then broke into a smile and bowed, stepping back.

She turned and walked over to James' grave, where he lay next to Skylar and hers.

She took a deep breath and went to Skylar's grave, placing snapdragons by her before stepping back.

"Skylar of the Lias, you are the first Lias, half or not, ever to be buried. But this should not separate you from the others buried in this graveyard. The Lias are independent creatures, wishing to be free to go wherever they want. You chose to stay tied down to James, because you love him. This is one of the most amazing acts I have ever had the pleasure of witnessing, and I respect you eternally for that. May you and James run free together in the sky.
James. My brother. Friend. Protector to all. You were a rebellious servant, who always wanted more. You showed me that there is so much more to life than being a maid, and that sometimes a little disobedience is the right thing to do. You also showed me how powerful love can be, family or not. Your love for Skylar will always stand as an example to us, and we will always remember you."
She turned, blinking back tears and walking away, leaving hundreds of thousands of tombstones. But only one other besides James and Skylar's stood out to her.

Regina and Max Orlan

She took a shaky breath and got to the top of the hill, where the crowd joined her.

"May you never be forgotten."

A Letter

Dearest Madrid,

I write in regret, knowing how disappointed you will be with me when I've told you what I've done. But you must not judge me harshly, for I was misguided and terribly nagged.

The monster known as Piland- you know the one- came to me in the night, and brought me outside to the forest far from our home.

He distracted me from my duty, and told me that our unborn child's life would be in danger from him. He angered me, and I wish to stop writing, I am embarrassed so.

He continued to build up my anger and stress that I could not hold it in- I dueled him, as he wanted for so many years to prove his powers.
The duel went on for hours, yet neither of us showed signs of weakness. I do not wish to brag, Mildred, when I say we were evenly matched.
We were not aware of the time passing or our surroundings, It was a battle between brothers, and we would not stop until one of us emerged victoriously. Neither became so.
Eventually, our powers met, and a blast formed, knocking us off our feet.
The blast cut through an entire section of the forest, and I never dare to enter there again after the tragedy that had befallen because of my foolish actions at that spot.
Both our powers split in two. I became injured and frail, so I apologize in advance for the lack of dances

I planned on presenting to our child to make him or her laugh.
My brother Piland was turned into a literal monster. He became a shapeshifter and has evacuated to a cave deep in the woods. I wonder what his wife Nala will think of this, now that she is with child.
I have heard now that he is spreading chaos amongst the other creatures of the forest, looking for worthy subjects to become his tribe.
I went home with difficulty in my new form, but the sight that awaited me did not ease my suffering. Mildred, I am crying now as I write this. As I reminisce your delicate frame on the floor, blood dripping into a sticky puddle you would have hated to get onto the floor you worked so hard on. I used to tell you to stop worrying about the floor and worry about yourself, but now I stare at the floor and see the beautiful designs you put into it, and I wish for nothing more but your life.

I have recently found where the other half of my powers have gone. A couple in the village have recently had twins– I could feel their aura of power from down the road. I hope only I was able to feel that, though. I plan on telling the parents as soon as I finish this letter, or they will be in much trouble indeed.

I cannot begin to describe my grief without you, Mildred. I hope that you will find in your love for me to forgive me, and to tell our child about his or her father while you wait for me in Heaven. I wish I could find a way to come now, but I'm afraid the twins are in more danger than I can imagine, and I must help, as I'm sure you would have wanted.

I hope to see you soon, Mildred, but for now, I must go.

With love,

Arbia

Made in the USA
Middletown, DE
26 October 2016